Mrs. Meyer's Magical Garden

A Novel.

I0680992

A PLEASURE TO READ

IN ALL SEASONS –

THE PICTURES CHANGE, THE STORY REMAINS.

riede auf Erden. Ich habe damals daran geglaubt.
der Hammelburg zurückkam, saßen in der Bürger-
Schminke. Sie hatten mich erwartet.
und nicht ohne Be-

Nikola Hahn

Mrs. Meyer's Magical Garden

A NOVEL.

Translated by Claudia Boulton

Bibliographic information of the German National Library:

The German National Library has registered this publication
in the German National Bibliography;
detailed bibliographic data available via the internet at http://dnb.dnb.de

Cover design and illustration: N. Hahn
Composition and Layout: N. Hahn
English translation copyright © 2015 by Claudia Boulton

First published in Germany under the title *Der Garten der alten Dame*
by Thoni Verlag, Rödermark © 2013 by Nikola Hahn
Printed by Amazon Distribution GmbH, Leipzig

ISBN 978-3-944177-46-5

For Thomas
Because you are here.

Someone who hears butterflies laughing
can tell how clouds taste.
Undisturbed by fear, he will discover night
beneath the moonlight.

(Carlo Karges, Novalis)

Autumn.

Omnium rerum principia parva sunt.
The beginnings of all things are small.

Marcus Tullius Cicero

CHAPTER ONE

The colourful leaves drifted gently down onto the pavement one by one, directly in front of the old villa's entrance. At least Eli presumed they did because to actually see the tree, she would have had to lean out of the window of her room which was not her room any more. She looked at the tree one last time: a gnarled English Oak. She knew that from Pa. That crooked wooden body had to be ancient, even older than the house, which was quite old too. Oh, Pa could really tell magnificent stories! Eli missed him already, even though they had not yet parted. He would accompany her to the new home, as Ma had gravely explained. Eli cringed when she felt his hand on her shoulder.

"So, it's goodbye to the old warrior is it, Ronia Robber?"

Eli held back her tears and turned to face him. "The old oak is going to grow another hundred years, even without me", she explained bravely.

Pa stroked her hair. She hated it when others did that, but coming from him she loved it. Just as she loved it when he called her Ronia. That was their great secret. Not even Ma knew that she was really and truly named after the heroine in Astrid Lindgren's story: Ronia the Robber's Daughter. She who lived in the crumbling Matt's Fort in dark Matt's Wood who was adventurous, brave and one of a kind. Just like Eli.

Pa had whispered that he had done this secretly as Ma would feel that Ronia was not the right name for a decent girl. She had mused for many an hour quite how he had managed this without Ma finding out, because eventually she always found everything out.

"E-li-sa-betha!" she heard the voice from the hallway. "We have to get going!"

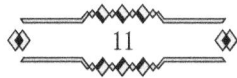

Eli did not like it when Ma stretched her name out like that. Actually, she did not want to be called Elisabetha at all. Eli was just about okay. If she could choose, she would have everyone call her just Ronia.

The door opened. Ma came in. She pulled a face. "I should have guessed that you two were dawdling again."

Pa just closed the window and said nothing.

The new school was really daft. In the classroom, the only free seat was next to a plump girl, bespectacled, with hair brushed awfully neatly, whose name was Emma and, to cap it all, regrettably lived nearby. Yes, Emma was just as daft as the whole school. And the teacher was daft and the new street and the new flat in the dull mouse grey box of an apartment building more so still. In fact, the whole area was daft: monochrome terraced houses, everywhere, all the same, each with an identical miniature garden or shabby concrete buildings, just as the one in which they now lived. *No trespassing!* a dented sign said, meaning the little patch of threadbare grass beside the entrance. Judging by the myriad of little brown heaps, the local dogs did not care a bit. There was not even an oak tree here! Eli could only see half the trees because the others were hidden behind the high wall across the street. Shrubs grew along this wall with an open space in front, unnaturally barren and with the mandatory prohibiting sign. Obviously they expected to build on it soon. The largest tree behind the wall had bright yellow leaves. They looked freshly painted. That yellow tree was about the only really beautiful thing in the whole street.

After school, Eli listlessly climbed the stairs to the new flat which was directly under the roof. She missed the creaking of her old wooden staircase, the shabby floor boards in the timeworn flat, the echoes in the corridor when someone spoke and those high airy ceilings with white stucco giving one the impression of living in a castle. Previously, Ma had never liked things to be scattered around, but now she did not seem to care.

The new corridor was narrow and dark. Even during the day, lights were needed to have any hope of seeing anything and the coats did not magically disappear behind mysterious gliding doors, but hung

helplessly in the open on a rickety coat rack. Eli hung up her jacket and went into her room: narrow alley-like with a small chink of a window looking onto the street. Eli opened it to let in some autumn sun. She missed Pa so much, it almost hurt.

"Now I have to pay everything double!" he had moaned whilst arguing with Ma about rent, heating cost and varied "other expenses". Even visiting rights had caused a squabble. Eli did not like it when her parents disagreed, but she supposed it was still preferable to them not speaking to each other at all.

Outside there was not much to see: a rusty old flower lattice in front of an empty windowsill and some dull weathered roofs. But the sky was beautifully blue and the sun projected fascinating patterns into the street. From beyond the high wall the yellow tree blazed across at her. Eli grinned. Since when did a wall impose an obstacle for Ronia? She would go straight away and have a closer look. Sadly Ma arrived home first.

The very next day Eli pretended to go home directly after school. But she actually waited behind the entrance door until she could be sure that she was rid of Emma. Luckily, no one was about when she left the house. Pretending to be bored she strolled across the barren area and inspected the wall. It was built of roughly trimmed stones, overgrown with moss and so high, that Eli was unable to see beyond it. In the town this type of wall surrounded rich people's gardens which was why Eli and her friend, Susi, had imagined being invisible and being able to just walk straight through them. The only way of gaining a glimpse of the inside was usually through the typical mighty wrought iron gates. But here there was no such thing, just an abundance of thorny bushes and terraced houses left and right. The piece of land beyond the wall seemed to be very large, the entrance probably from the street parallel.

It took Eli a while to find the right turning only to be disappointed to find the gate blocked-off with rush mats. These bore the ubiquitous *No trespassing!* sign and below *Parents are responsible for their children!* This was obviously a clue of curious things yet to be discovered and therefore well worth the risk of looking for an opening to

sneak in. Susi also thought the same; the reason why they had been in trouble a short time previously. First with the owner of the house, then with Ma and finally that evening with Pa on his return home from work. Of course, that did not change the fact that such signs were a deliberate siren call for the inquisitive. The art was obviously just not to be caught in the act. So Eli decided to stand on tiptoe, but that did not help. The garden behind the wall remained hidden.

"You better go away!" someone called out from behind her. She was startled and turned around. It was plump Emma, had she followed secretly?

"Why?" Eli asked.

"'Cause it's forbidden."

"Have you been in?"

"Of course not!"

Eli thought of Susi and turned to leave.

"Where are you going?" Emma asked.

"Home."

"May I come along with you for a bit?"

Eli shrugged and strolled nonchalantly off down the street. Emma tried to keep up whilst maintaining a steady stream of chitchat. She talked of school and how she could help Eli with her homework, but Eli was not listening. She was with the lovely yellow tree and wondering how she could get into the garden. Eli stopped and looked at Emma.

"Aren't you just a little bit curious?"

"About what?" the plump girl asked.

"Well, what really happens behind that wall!"

Emma pulled a face. "Just loads of weeds and a tired tumble-down old house."

"So you have been in!" Eli exclaimed.

"No, well yes, okay ... old Mrs. Meyer used to live there, but she died. And my mummy says it's about time that they got rid of that eyesore." She sounded as if she would be even happier than her mummy about the demolition and from that moment on, Eli was sure that Emma was definitely not going to be her friend. Anyway, she no longer wanted a friend. And, besides, she would prefer to be

completely by herself in this world. Then at least she would not have to feel sad when all the others were no longer around. Maybe she could go and search for Matt's Fort with Pa next weekend?

"I'm glad we're in the same class", Emma said.

Eli thought, I'm not, and left. When she got back home, Ma had not yet returned. Her mother now had to work, but she was happy to be free. At least that was what she told her friend Bridget on the phone. Eli did not feel free; more like trapped in her little room. Although, on reflection, it was not really that small compared to Ma's.

"I only need it as a sleeping space", she had explained smiling. "But you definitely need a proper space to do your homework."

This proper space was a niche below the window, just about large enough to take Eli's desk. When she looked up from her homework and ignored the ugly rusting lattice, Eli looked directly at the sky. And if she stood up, she could see the street and the wall opposite with assorted colourful bushes behind – and of course the yellow tree which shone like a beam of promise: Ronia was definitely going to find the entrance and courageously explore all that was be found in that old Mrs. Meyer's garden! Now she just had to be careful not to run into Emma.

Unfortunately, this was more easily said than done as Emma seemed overjoyed to have finally found someone whose nerves she could test on a regular basis. Eli did not like her, but she could not bring herself to show her aversion more openly than she had done already. So she was forced to endure Emma's tedious chitchat every morning on her way to school and every afternoon on her way back, always giving a sigh of relief when they finally said goodbye. Emma lived with her parents in one of those dull terraced houses bordering the wall of Mrs. Meyer's garden, indeed this was the sole reason why Eli had finally agreed to tag along and take a look at her room in the first place. Similar to her own, it was located under the roof, but what a difference: Emma's room was large and bright and even had its own little balcony from which you could gaze into Mrs. Meyer's garden! Actually, you could only guess what was there because trees, shrubs and bamboo blocked the view. Eli could merely make out a small part of an ancient roof between the abundant autumn colours.

"Did Mrs. Meyer live on her own?" Eli asked.

Emma shrugged. "No idea. I was still little when she died. My mummy says she was odd."

"Why didn't you ever invite her over for a piece of cake?"

"We didn't know her and anyway, people said it was better not to get involved with her."

"But why?" insisted Eli.

"Oh, what do I know!" shrugged Emma and looked at Eli slowly shaking her head.

"Why are you so interested? She died ages ago."

Eli remembered the story about an ancient garden that Pa used to read to her, with an old lady who declared that the flowers were her children and of all the good garden spirits who had wanted to help. Eli had longed to know how a good garden spirit looked. Not even Pa had been able to tell her that. Maybe one of them was hiding in Mrs. Meyer's garden?

"Want t' play with my dolls?" Emma asked bluntly.

Eli shook her head. "No. I've got to go home."

Ambling down the street she started to whistle. Something she had learned from Pa.

"You teach that child all kinds of mischief", Ma had exclaimed, but she had been smiling when she said it. That had been long ago, but Eli could remember exactly that it had been on a warm sunny Saturday afternoon. They had visited Elephants in the zoo and on returning home a shiny blackbird had sat singing in the oak tree.

"Can you do that, too?" Pa had asked. "Whistle like a bird!?" And then he had shown her how; she copied him and the blackbird had joined in. And then a brown one came along and even managed to whistle with a mouth full of worms, and Pa had said sternly: "One doesn't sing with one's beak full!" Eli laughed so loudly that the blackbird became scared and flew away and the brown one almost dropped its worms, but managed to disappear into the wild vines to feed her little ones.

Eli had reached the barren piece of land and strolled in an openly nonchalant way past the prohibiting signs towards the wall. She was just about to inspect the shrubbery, when she heard a familiar voice.

"You are going to be in real trouble when they catch you!" Emma pointed demonstrably at the sign and looked at Eli in the same way Ma used to look when she had done something particularly naughty. She offered Eli a lollypop. "Like one? Raspberry flavour."

"Just leave me alone!" snapped Eli.

Emma's eyes filled with tears.

A cry-baby, on top of everything else! Eli thought about continuing regardless, but this awful Emma would surely squeal on her.

"See yer", she said and left.

It took an awfully long time until Saturday finally came around. Pa picked Eli up after breakfast. She had hoped that the three of them would go out and do something together, but Ma did not react to Pa's presence in any way. And so it was that the two of them drove into town by themselves. Despite being snubbed by mum, Pa was in good spirits and he invited Eli to an ice cream parlour. The ice cream tasted excellent, but not as good as it had when Ma had been with them. Eli had been looking forward to see Pa and now that he was here she missed Ma.

"Shall we go to the zoo?" he asked. She shook her head and wished herself far away.

On Sunday morning it rained. Through all the greyness Eli had difficulty making out the glowing yellow tree behind the wall. When she leant out of the window, water from the broken drain pipe splashed onto her face and she vowed that as soon as it stopped raining Ronia would go into Mrs. Meyer's garden – no matter what!

Two days later the sun shone again and not even Emma could stop her because she was in bed with the flu.

"Don't you think you should go and visit your new friend?" Ma asked.

"She's not my friend!"

"She is a very nice girl", Ma said. How would she know? She had only ever seen her twice! Anyway, Eli had the impression Ma did not pay attention to what she was saying as much as she had done whilst they still lived in town. Sometimes she even forgot her promises. The

telephone calls to Bridget also became shorter. Eli imagined being free would be different.

"Well okay", she gave in. "I'll visit Emma."

The visit was a short one. Eli said that she had something important to attend to which, strictly speaking, was not even a lie.

When Eli sneaked across the barren space this time she carefully looked around, but there were only a few people about and no one was taking any notice of her. She followed the wall to the right until she reached some thorny bushes. Somewhere behind was Emma's parents' garden, but there was no way of getting through. Eli walked in the other direction but there, too, the wall disappeared into impenetrable shrubbery.

After searching intensively, Eli managed to find a spot with almost no thorns. She fought her way through and unexpectedly ended up in a kind of natural tent: spindly branches and thorny tendrils formed a hollow, the back of which was formed by the wall. In one place a few stones were missing and the gap was just big enough for Eli to fit through. She was so happy, she almost clapped her hands. The stones felt cool and were covered in soft moss. It smelled of earth, leaves and mushrooms. As with the near side, the far side of the wall was covered by tall shrubs preventing access. If you were not specifically looking for it, there would be no way you could find it.

Eli looked around curiously. Everywhere trees glowed in rich, warm colours. The grass was knee-high and in a weed-choked bed there were flowers in bloom of which she did not even know the names.

The radiant yellow tree stood close to a house which had almost completely disappeared under ivy and thorny branches. Wooden stairs led to a covered patio where Eli noticed two faded wicker chairs and a table. And a rocking chair that moved.

"Good afternoon, Elisabetha. Or should I say Ronia? How nice of you to visit me."

Eli was startled and stared at the old woman who sat in the rocking chair. She was wrapped in a blue and red check blanket on which her hands rested like shrivelled winter apples in spring. Her face resembled a map of creases and wrinkles and her white hair was

twisted into an intricate knot. At least Eli presumed so, as she could not actually see it but Grandma Mary used to do her hair like that.

"Please ... I'm sorry", she stuttered. "I'm terribly sorry. I ..."

The wrinkles seemed to be amused.

Eli paused. "How come you know my name?"

"That's my little secret. Two names – that's really tiring. So, what should I call you?"

"My Ma says Elisabetha. My Pa says Ronia, but only in secret. Everyone else calls me Eli."

"And what's your favourite?"

No one had ever asked her that. "Well ... Whichever you like."

"No. You decide, my dear child."

Eli actually hated it when people called her *dear child*, but the old lady made it sound like an honour. Eli debated if Pa might agree if a stranger called her by her secret name. Probably not. She climbed up the steps. The creaking sounded familiar. "Alright, Eli. And what's your name?"

"I'm Mrs. Meyer. But if you like you can call me Auntie Mildred."

Calling perfect strangers Auntie was even worse that being a *dear child*. "I'll call you Mrs. Meyer."

Mrs. Meyer pointed to the wicker chair; Eli sat down hesitantly. "Emma says you died."

"Well, well. So that's what your friend says, is it?"

"She isn't my friend."

"And why not?"

"Because!"

Mrs. Meyer's wrinkles were enormously amused.

"Why are you not telling me off?"

"Why should I?"

"Because I, ... well, climbed into your garden.",

"This isn't my garden."

"But, ... don't you live here?"

"I'm only visiting."

Eli looked towards the open patio door. "Then who?"

The old lady lightly put her index finger to her and whispered: "You'll see."

Eli felt herself getting goose bumps. This Mrs. Meyer was nice enough, but at the same time a little peculiar. She remembered how Ma had always warned her not to get involved with strangers and that terrible things might happen if she did. But Ma had talked about men, not women and surely did not mean old ladies such as Mrs. Meyer. Eli thought that anyway at a pinch she could run away. Mrs. Meyer surely was not very steady on her feet. On the other hand: she would not harm her, would she?

"Have you got a husband?"

Her wrinkles twinkled. "Oh yes! Well, I had one, a while ago."

"Did you get divorced?"

"Oh no, Otto and I were married for sixty-six years. And then he died."

Eli tried to work out how old someone must be to be able to be married for such a long time. Grandma Mary died when she was sixty-three and she had been married to Grandpa Friedhelm, but he had died such a long time ago that Eli only knew him from photographs. And Grandma Augusta was sixty-five and had raised her child, Ma, quite comfortably without a chap, which she proudly pointed out every time she visited. And Ma? She had not even managed ten years with Pa... Could someone really be married for sixty-six years?

"Do you have children?"

Mrs. Meyer nodded. "Two daughters and a son, but they live far from here."

"Aren't you sad to be all on your own?"

"But you are here."

"I'll leave soon."

"You will come back."

"How do you know?"

She smiled. "You'll see."

CHAPTER TWO

As soon as Eli could think clearly, she found herself in her room at her desk. Through the rust-stained flower-lattice-grey she gazed at the orange-red painted sunset-sky. Old Mrs. Meyer had talked a little nonsense, but Grandma Mary had done the same and Eli had loved her anyway. She had felt a great sense of comfort and security, inside in winter on the stove bench, outside in summer between the beds with myriads of colourful flowers. Grandma Mary even grew vegetables; carrots and lettuce and radishes and even herbs that had a lovely aroma and tasted even better. And all those many goodies! The raspberries and strawberries Eli used to nibble directly from the bush, the nuts that tumbled from the tree in autumn and apples that needed to be stored in the cellar for a little while and smelled of sun and summery earth even in the depth of winter. And then, one day, Pa had come home and said Grandma Mary now lived with the dear Lord in his heavenly garden. Eli had not understood, and it seemed Pa did not either, because instead of answering her questions, he had read her the story of the old garden.

Grandma Mary's garden had had everything, except cherries. She had said that a cherry tree would be too big, and for a proper harvest you needed at least two. But in her previous garden she had had one and her neighbour next door had one too so they harvested buckets full of sumptuous red cherries every summer. Eli opened a tattered book which she had often read with Pa and looked at the pictures. One could find lots of clever answers to important questions in it. For example, where elephants came from or why it rains or even which trees grow in Germany and what their leaves look like. Eli smiled when she saw the illustration of the English oak tree. She kept browsing – and indeed: the yellow tree was a cherry! Grandma Mary

had often said that Pa had climbed into the cherry tree every summer and nibbled the cherries just like Eli had done with the berries. Only she did not have to climb for them. Pa had eaten so many cherries that he got tummy-ache. And he had cherry stone spitting competitions with the neighbour's boy.

"Your grandma didn't like that at all", Pa had said. "Although I always won." He had grinned when he said that and actually looked a bit like a naughty little boy.

"Why did you move from your former garden?" Eli wanted to know.

Pa looked sad. "Sometimes you have to leave a place you love because circumstances force it upon you."

Eli wondered aloud how circumstances managed to do this, but no one was able to give her a proper answer. Around that time, Pa sometimes looked sad and so did Ma and they either fought or did not talk at all. Eli suspected that something terrible might happen and that they might separate as her friend Susi's parents had done; hoping at the same that it would not come to that. And then it did happen after all and she had to leave her beautiful room just like Pa once had to leave the cherry tree garden. And yet, Grandma Mary had not divorced!

Eli closed the book and looked out of the window. The sky now seemed as rusty as the lattice and then all colour disappeared and the yellow tree turned grey. *It is about time they got rid of that eyesore,* she remembered Emma's words. How could someone say something so mean? And on top of that they had lied: Mrs. Meyer was not dead at all! And as long as she lived, no one could destroy her garden – or could they? Anyway, Eli preferred not to imagine what it would be like to look out of the window in the morning and not see the blazing yellow tree any more. Suddenly she had to laugh! Dearie me! She had totally forgotten that flowers and trees could fend for themselves and chase nasty people away! But she only knew that because Pa had told her the story of the old garden.

In this, the old garden was so large, no one knew exactly where it ended because it lay in the middle of meadows and woods and it did not have a fence. There were mighty trees and colourful flowers and a house where a couple lived with their children. The years passed

and when the children had grown up and moved away, the parents stayed behind. The town with its houses and streets kept squeezing in closer to the old garden and the parents, who were now grandparents, had a big wall built, so the trees and flowers would not be eaten by the town. When the old people died, the town had long surrounded the walls and garden and ate into the countryside beyond. No one had wanted the house, so they pulled it down and built an ugly block of flats in its place. Between the remaining garden and the block of flats they put a fence and again the years passed. The town grew into a city and the ugly block of flats became uglier and the old garden lay quietly behind the fence like a desert island in an ocean of houses

One day, a boy with his little sister and his parents moved into the ugly block of flats. From their window, the children could see the old garden and imagined what it would be like to play in it. The other children had told them a nasty gardener lived behind the fence and so no one dared venture in.

But the boy was brave and made a plan to outwit the gardener. Indeed, both siblings managed to get into the garden without being seen and when they found no one there, they turned to mischief. They ripped leaves from the trees and trampled on the flowers; they turned beetles onto their backs to make them wriggle, they tore down spiders' webs and threw stones at the birds and caused much desolation all around. When it got dark however, they could not find their way back out and suddenly the old garden came to life: the animals could speak and the flower spirits rose and together they decided that the children had to die for their cruel acts. That's when Eli became really scared, because even though the boy and his little sister had been quite nasty, she felt pity for the two and was relieved when the beech fairy granted their wish. She shrank the children until they were teeny-weeny and sent them on an adventurous and dangerous trip beneath the earth. They visited the earth mother, met the father of the oceans and were guests in the Tower of Winds. From there, they finally flew to the old lady's garden who called the flowers her children and where the good garden spirits lived.

And a little later they were very nearly eaten by greedy mice. But only nearly.

The story of the old garden was at once exciting and creepy, but also funny and a little sad and when Pa had finished reading it, he had to immediately start all over again, and then for a third time. After that, he refused to read it any more. After all, there were other interesting stories. That was quite true, but the children's experiences were just as exciting as Ronia's adventures in Matt's Wood and Pa had had to read that one so many times until Eli knew it by heart. As he left, through the window, she could heard the wind whispering in the oak tree and she ceased to be Eli; she was Ronia. Through the dark Matt's Wood she ran to the old garden. The boy and his sister were waiting for her and together they climbed up the cherry tree, all the way up to the highest branch where the biggest and sweetest fruit hung. And then they chewed as noisily as they possibly could and laughed and spat the stones skywards.

"Eli – you're not supposed to dream, do your homework instead!" Alarmed, Eli looked towards the door.

"Dinner's ready", Ma said. She looked tired.

The following day was a "Lateautumnpicturebookthursday" as Pa would put it. The sun shone from an electric blue sky and Eli looked out from her school desk. Emma slid a little note over, but Eli pretended not to see it.

"Want t' play with my new doll?" Emma asked on the way home.

Whenever she was not busy solving mathematics problems, Emma could dress and undress Barbie dolls for hours on end. Eli hated Barbie dolls, but hated maths even more. But most of all she hated Emma! Simply because she was constantly pestering Eli so she was unable to go into Mrs. Meyer's garden. Eli had thought about telling her everything, but decided against it. It was her big secret that Mrs. Meyer was still alive. Suddenly she had an idea on how to get rid of Emma. She put on an apologetic expression and explained that she would not be able to come out to play because she had to go to tennis. Emma hated anything and everything to do with sport or exercise in general. Predictably, she immediately pulled a face.

"I am starting to take regular lessons now", said Eli. "With my own personal coach." She had no idea what a personal coach was, but it was

exactly what Bridget had said yesterday evening and Ma had explained she did not have money to waste on such frippery. Somehow Bridget did not seem to appreciate this judgement and did not stay long.

"What a pity", said Emma.

Eli was glad her trick had worked. All she now needed was to wait for the right moment to creep into the garden. She squeezed through the gap in the wall, her heart thumping. Would Mrs. Meyer still be sat in her rocking chair?

She was. "I'm glad you're visiting me", she said, repeating her previous days greeting.

"I'm happy, too", Eli said.

"And why then do you look as you do?"

Eli peeked in the direction of Emma's balcony. What if that silly-billy found out that instead of practising tennis with her coach she was sitting on the terrace with the not-so-dead Mrs. Meyer? As if the old lady could read her thoughts she said: "Don't worry, this garden is so overgrown, no one can see in from outside. And if we don't talk too loudly, no one is going to hear us either." She lowered her voice. "We are in a forbidden world."

Eli had no idea what Mrs. Meyer was talking about. She pointed at the blazing yellow tree whose coat of leaves had thinned out quite a bit. "That's a cherry tree, right?"

"You wished for a cherry tree", Mrs. Meyer said, as if it was the most natural thing in the world that wishes came true immediately.

"This tree is only here because I wished for it?"

Mrs Meyer shook her head. "It was already standing here when I was your age."

"You know what I wish for even more? That Ma and Pa don't fight any longer and that we all live happily together again."

The old lady smiled, but this time her wrinkles did not join in. "There are things that are and things that will be. But there are also things that aren't and won't ever be. I think Nick's calling."

"Who's Nick?" Eli asked.

"He's over there, the old lazybones." She said it in a way which made you feel that there was nothing more endearing than an old lazybones. "I'm sure he'd be very happy if you went and said hello to him."

Eli skipped down the terrace steps and ran over to the cherry tree in curiosity. The trunk was covered in ivy; here and there a little cracked bark peered out from between the green tendrils.

"A wondrous dream, my pretty tree", something hummed from somewhere. The humming was followed by a chuckle. "You have to walk around the trunk."

Eli did as she was told. Between the ferns a little oversized gnome lounged in the sparse grass. It looked to Eli as if she had just woken him from a nap. His grey hands lay folded in his lap and his grey pointed cap had slipped over his grey face. On his grey trousers he had a grey patch and when Eli looked closer she saw that the whole creature was of weathered grey stone. "How come you can talk?" she asked flabbergasted.

"Why not?" he replied.

"Who are you?"

"My name is Nicodemus. I'm a Troll. But if you like, you may call me Nick."

Eli was startled. A dark Troll? Here? That was impossible! "Trolls live in Sweden or Norway."

Nick chuckled and Eli began to feel insecure. "Pa says that and he knows!"

"Maybe. But sometimes we move."

Eli remembered Mrs. Meyer's words. "I didn't wish for a Troll."

"I beg your pardon! Do you really think I have to rely on your wishing to be here?"

"So why are you here then?"

"I'm enjoying the sun."

"You're sitting in the shade", Eli noted.

Nick rocked his grey head. "How could I enjoy the sun if it burns my plaster? I watch it rise in the morning and set in the evening. I watch it wander from East to West, how it paints the sky, how it throws patterns of light on leaves and flowers."

"And what do you do when the sun doesn't shine?"

"Then I watch the clouds: how little white lambs turn into white sheep, how they flock together and drift apart until they are dull and grey and race across the sky. And then I count the raindrops that drip off the leaves and I'm happy when the sun begins to shine again."

Eli sat down beside him. "Are you a good garden spirit then?"

Nick chortled. "My wardrobe contains a little too much stone for a spirit, don't you think?"

Eli joined in and laughed. "So what else do you do?"

"Think."

"About what?"

"About the virtues of a wise gardener"

"What's a wise gardener?"

"What you should be asking is: What does a wise gardener do?"

"So. What does he do?"

"Only the necessary."

"And what does that mean?"

Nick looked at his folded hands. "A wise gardener allows himself time to watch the flowers bloom. Listen to the bees humming and the flight of the butterflies."

"You can't hear butterflies!"

"If you're quiet, you can hear everything."

Eli leaned against the tree. "I don't hear a thing!"

"How do you want to hear whilst you're talking so much?"

"But-"

"Shhh..."

A colourful butterfly landed on a flower. Eli saw how it unrolled a thin tongue. She sat still and watched how it drank the nectar. It opened and closed its wings, opened them once again and fluttered off. Was there not a soft shimmering vibration in the air, a gentle hint of flapping?

Nick smiled. "Well?"

"I'm sure I just imagined it."

"What makes you so sure you just imagined it?"

Eli shrugged. The Troll winked at her. "Maybe because every rational human being knows that one cannot hear butterflies fly?"

"Exactly!" But she was not satisfied with her own answer.

When Eli returned to the garden the next day, she hastily greeted Mrs. Meyer and then ran straight over to Nick who was dozing amongst the ferns.

She crouched down. "Tell me, don't you sometimes feel bored?"

"What is it: bored?"

"You don't know what boredom is – when everything is dull and slow?" Eli asked puzzled.

He thought for a moment. "Dull, slow ... well, yes, I know about those things. I love to watch the snow slowly falling on a dull day and how it covers all the flower beds, and I am happy when after a while it slowly melts and then it takes quite a while until the ferns slowly unfurl and conjure a dull and shady little place for me which doesn't really matter because in spring the sun is not so strong anyway. And in summer I wait again for a long time until the leaves slowly start falling in autumn and then I like to gaze around especially slowly at all the different colours."

Eli laughed. This strange Troll really did not seem to know what she was talking about.

"Boredom means that I am bored. That I don't have anything to do, that ..." She stopped. It was difficult to explain being bored to someone who doesn't know the feeling.

Nick nodded. "Yes. Being bored is wonderful."

"No", Eli shouted. "Being bored is awful! Because you just sit around stupidly and ..."

"Now I understand", Nick interrupted her cheerily. "My boredom is wonderful, because I sit around cleverly."

Eli gave up. Quietly they sat side by side and as soon as a leaf fluttered down from the tree, Nick watched with great interest. Hesitantly, Eli followed his example and indeed: each one had its own shape and colour. One was a browny yellow-red and heart shaped, another one looked like a yellow dotted drop, a third one was redbrowngreenyellow, a fourth lightochreyellowgreen with chocolate-marshmallow sprinkles on it; some were undamaged, others had jagged tears, round, angled, small and large holes through which the autumn sun twinkled and with others the corners and edges were missing.

Nick explained that they had all grown from thick round buds in May and in the June sun they had changed from their light green spring clothes into their rich green summer costumes. He enthused

about the juicy crisp-red cherries so much that Eli's mouth started to water. At last he revealed that the inside of those small and large holes had ended up as the favourite dish in countless insects' stomachs and that a lot of those insects were moving into the colourful heap of leaves in the garden as their wintering grounds. The troll chatted without moving: his back leaned against the tree, legs crossed, hands folded in his lap, the grey pointed cap over his grey forehead.

An unobservant visitor might have thought he was sleeping, but Eli knew that he was actually explaining all this at this moment. It was getting quite late when she returned to the terrace. Mrs. Meyer was watering some flowers.

"Even though I didn't wish for Nick", Eli said. "I am really glad he's here."

The old lady smiled. "Wait until you meet Rudy."

"Who's Rudy?"

"You'll see. Would you like some mint tea?"

"Oh yes please!"

"Then let's pick some." She put the watering can away and Eli followed her inquisitively behind the house. She stopped in front of a bed by the wall on which the evening sun shone. At the foot of the wall the earth was damp and from there dense green bunches of plants grew across the path neighbouring the lawn.

"That's a bit cheeky that mint: once it feels at home one can't get rid of it quickly", Mrs. Meyer said. "Well, I suppose if you smell that good you are allowed to be a bit cheeky, don't you think?" Carefully she guided Eli's hand across the leaves. The scent reminded her of chewing gum, but there was something else: a hint of fruit – and cinnamon? "It's ginger mint", the old lady explained. "But you can also have your tea with banana, strawberry or orange flavour. Or would you prefer it pure and simple?"

"With strawberry flavour!" Eli said in delight and gently plucked the leaves from their stalks as reverently as if they were made of gold.

"What's the smell in here?" Ma asked when she got home that evening.

Eli beamed. "Mint!" She told her they had been out with their biology teacher and that they had found lots of mint plants in a large overgrown garden that no one looked after. And she had taken a few leaves with her because they smelled so delicious.

And, in a way, that was true.

CHAPTER THREE

After her third visit to Nick and Mrs. Meyer Eli decided it was about time not to be afraid of the forbidden garden anymore. Because in reality she was Ronia, it was obvious that she should practise not being afraid of something in the same way the brave robber's daughter did in Matt's Wood: by practising until she was really good at it, she was finally not afraid any more. So from now on, Eli crept in to the old garden as often as she possibly could. She would have liked to practise daily, but that did not work because of Emma.

Even she would have not believed in daily tennis lessons. Just in case, Eli made up a few more excuses and she told Ma that she had been doing homework with her new friend. That way she could practice not being afraid of the old garden more often and each and every time there was something interesting to see, hear or feel – and most importantly taste: delicious strawberry-mint tea on Mrs. Meyer's terrace for example. And afterwards she always visited Nick.

"Why are you sitting under the cherry tree?"

He yawned and his pointed cap started sliding. "Because I can lounge comfortably here."

"You could lounge just as well on the terrace and it's shady over there."

He straightened his cap. "I'm sitting quite comfortably here thank you. Why should I change that?"

Eli had the feeling he was grinning inwardly. "You're right, a stone troll can't wander around."

Now he actually grinned from one grey ear to the other. "What a great excuse!"

Eli shook her head and left him crouched under the tree. And the more she thought about it: the more she knew that's where he belonged.

The old garden offered a multitude of surprises: a secret pavilion, overgrown with thorns for example and a pond which was actually rather more a lake. Bushy grass grew on the opposite bank, this side was swampy and lined with ferns. A little stream gurgled over mossy stones, it probably originated from somewhere behind the thorns by the pavilion.

Eli walked around the lake and was startled when right in front of her a fat brown frog jumped into the water. The pavilion's window panes were tarnished and the door was stuck, but with a little push Eli was able to prise it open. Inside it smelt musty. Gardening tools hung on the back wall and in the middle a few wooden chairs were grouped around a table with a faded blue cloth. Surely it was lovely here in summer, but now the dim room seemed eerie. With a slight shudder Eli pulled the door shut.

Every morning Emma waited for Eli in front of the house that they could walk to school together. Eli would have preferred to walk alone; on the other hand it was quite useful if Ma saw her regularly with her alleged new friend although Emma was really the last person Eli wanted to be friends with. Anyway she had some friends: Mrs. Meyer and Nick. And if she ever wanted to have a best friend again it would surely not be someone like Emma who was so good and well-behaved that she did not even think of anything that was forbidden. No one liked her at school either, even though she let Eli and the others copy her homework. But what good was it, if apart from that she always said boring things and was every teacher's pet? On top of that, she still insisted Mrs. Meyer was dead, which was definitely not true. By now, Eli was convinced that Emma had not lied to her on purpose, she was just stupid and knew no better.

As much as Eli liked to be in the old garden during the week, she still looked forward to Saturdays when Pa picked her up, although being with him now was different than before. His flat was in the centre of town and it was even smaller and more uncomfortable than her and

Ma's. Pa said that this was the best for everyone, but he did not look as if he really believed it. And it was not true! The best had been their beautiful old flat and the warm feeling when Eli came home after school. There had always been something delicious to eat and Ma had helped her with homework. After that she had sometimes played the piano, baked a yummy cake and invited Bridget round. Now she did not have time for that. Neither did she have time for other things. Lighting candles. Reading books. Going for walks. Laughing. Neither did Pa.

"You're such a big girl now", he said when Eli asked him to read a story and he nowadays rarely called her Ronia Robber. Eli saw him, she heard him, but he was still far away from her; or was it that she was far away from him? He said: "It's nice you found a new friend." Ma had told him.

"Yes. Emma is a really nice friend", Eli said.

Although Pa was not listening as attentively as before, she was still happy with every minute she could spend with him. But she was just as happy that she had found the old garden. Whenever Eli thought of the garden she could smell the mint; she saw the reflection of the trees and shrubs in the pond between wilted water lily leaves, she felt the moss that was as soft as velvet. And from the cherry tree she could hear the black birds whistle like naughty boys. And so the forbidden garden turned into Ronia's wild forest and Mrs. Meyer's house became Matt's Fort. Although the old lady did not look at all like a robber.

Soon the days became shorter and the nights were cold and in the morning the streets and houses were wrapped in fog. One October morning several lessons were cancelled and as Emma and Eli walked back from school, wisps of fog still lingered in the air.

"Want to do homework together?" Emma asked.

"I have to go to tennis", Eli said.

Emma looked sad but did not say anything. Eli waited until she was out of sight. She even felt a little sorry for her. Somehow she was actually quite nice – if she were just not so terribly boring! She would not have survived a single day in Matt's Wood. Eli slid through the

gap in the wall and stopped in surprise: the old garden was like a magic kingdom! A cotton wool blanket spread across the grass and pond, soft white cobwebs were woven into the shrubs and trees and the flowers looked as though they had been painted over with milk. It was as quiet as if someone had stopped all time. Eli ran towards Nick. He put his index finger gently to his lips. She nodded and sat down. And so they sat together quietly and looked at the garden. Slowly the fog lightened; the sun broke through and the cotton wool cover dissolved into an airy veil. Colours, smells and sounds returned: leaves rustled, birds chirped and the white webs turned silver and the sun embroidered them with sparkling pearls.

"How beautiful!" Eli cried.

Nick smiled and said nothing.

"Indian Summer or Old Women's Summer", Mrs. Meyer explained when Eli arrived at the terrace. The old lady wore a thick jacket and sat in her rocking chair as usual.

"Why is it called that?" Eli wanted to know.

"Because what's disappearing glows just one last time in the fading light before its ultimate farewell." She smiled and all wrinkles in her face smiled with her. "This year the old women are quite late. Just like me."

"But you're not leaving are you?" Eli asked.

"Somehow, yes."

Eli put her hands on her hips as Ma did when she disliked something very profoundly. "I won't allow it!"

Mrs. Meyer laughed. Eli had an idea. "How would you feel if I moved in with you?"

She did not wait for an answer but ran back home. Ma looked at her a little strangely, then she said yes and quickly packed two suitcases. Together, they went to the front entrance of Mrs. Meyer's house. The iron gates were ajar and Mrs. Meyer was already there, waiting for them. Smiling, she took one suitcase from Ma and invited her onto the terrace.

It smelled of coffee, chocolate cake and mint tea. Pa sat in Mrs. Meyer's rocking chair and laughed. Ma laughed too and kissed him. Together they ate up the chocolate cake and Ma helped Mrs. Meyer

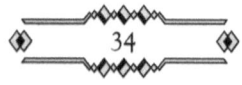

clearing up. Eli went to the cherry tree with Pa. Nick straightened his pointed cap and his grey hand politely shook Pa's. And then they climbed up to the highest branch and filled their stomachs with juicy cherries and then –

"That's not possible."

Mrs. Meyer had woken Eli from her dreams; she felt tired and sad. "Why not?"

"I think Rudy's calling."

"And who's Rudy?"

"You haven't met Rudy yet? Even though you've been to the pond so many times?"

Eli shook her head.

"Look by the old tree stump", Mrs. Meyer recommended.

Her sadness dissolved like the fog. Eli ran to the pond, squatted down and inspected the mossy stump by the swampy bank. What kind of tree must have once stood here? The dead roots were intertwined and reached into the water. They looked mysterious, but Eli could not detect anything that might have been called Rudy. Maybe Mrs. Meyer meant the fat frog that had jumped across her path the other day? But Eli had called him Kasimir and if she remembered correctly, she had told Mrs. Meyer about it.

Disappointed, Eli got up and was about to go back to the terrace when she heard a noise. At least she thought she heard it; maybe it was just the wind?

"Trillala, Trullala" sounded from the stump. That was definitely not the wind.

So squatting down again, she stared intensely into the intertwined roots. "Rudy?"

"Oh, please!" came back, seemingly annoyed, but this time very clearly. "I attach great importance to being called by my proper name!"

Eli almost fell into the pond with shock. She stared alternately between the roots and into the water, but she could still not see anything apart from her mirror image, dark green moss and lots of pickerelweed and watercress that seemed to be competing with each other for space. "Who are you?" she called. "And more importantly: where are you?"

"I am Earl Luitpold Rudolphius Ordinarius of Waggoner and I am generally well-known, everywhere!" a voice sounded indignantly from the stump.

"That's nice", said Eli. "But I can't see you."

"Then look properly!"

Indeed: a tiny red snake with a minute black head crept over the moss, but when Eli looked closer she was surprised to see that it was not a snake at all, but a tiny train. Pulled by a steam engine without steam, a coal tender without coal and a rusty red carriage with blue and white cheque curtains in tiny windows. She only knew about coal tenders and steam because Pa had read her the story of Luke the Train Driver and afterwards she had always bombarded him with questions. The trains that she had actually travelled on looked totally different and did not need coal. Anyway: what she saw could not be true! Eli thought about which snakes lived near ponds. Maybe a slowworm? But Pa had told her that a slowworm was not a snake, it just looked like one. And anyway, it was not red. "Are you a special slowworm?" she asked.

"Now, that's really the limit!" it grumbled from the moss. "I am not slow and I am not a worm! And I most certainly do not wish to be called Rudy!"

Oh dear, someone must have got hold of the wrong end of the stick. Eli laughed. "No, no! A slowworm is an animal that looks like a snake, but isn't one and it looks just like you. And Mrs. Meyer told me your name."

"I don't understand, but it sounds like an honest answer to me", Rudy said. He stopped and Eli almost supposed she had heard the sound of squeaking brakes, but of course that was nonsense.

"I have a big secret", Rudy said conspiratorially. "From the outside, I look like a pathetic little train, but actually I am a magnificent ship."

Then it was Eli's turn not to understand. "But such little trains don't exist."

"Well, as you can see very well, they do."

"Will you be terribly angry with me if I admit that I cannot remember your long name?"

"Acquaintances may call me Earl Luigi. Friends say Luigi. You may choose", he said patronisingly.

"How did you come to be in this garden?" Eli asked. "There are no rail tracks."

"And how did you get in here? There are no roads."

That was true. "Why are you so small?"

"Small?" Now Luigi-Rudy became really annoyed. "I am the largest ship in the world and I can sail across all seas!"

"How can you be a ship if you are a train with such a beautiful carriage? And anyway: where's the steam?"

"You find my carriage beautiful?" said Luigi-Rudy, sounding touched.

Eli nodded. "Especially the curtains. Will you tell me, why you want to be a ship so badly?"

"I don't want to be a ship, I am one", he said with utter conviction and for a moment Eli saw a proud three-master in front of her which sailed silently across an endless ocean. "I am a ship because it's fun to be a ship."

"And being a train isn't?"

"Nope. Going along the same tracks day in and day out, that's terribly boring. But a ship with its big white sails can criss-cross everywhere to the end of the world and even across the clouds to the sun. I am also an airship and I can build you a pretty castle if you wish."

That little train was a bit too big for its boots, Eli reckoned – but funny! And so Eli quietly christened him Luigi the funny locomotive. "Can I come along?" she asked and did not even think for a second about how she was going to fit into the tiny carriage.

"Of course." Luigi-Rudy made the door spring open.

Eli laughed because this time she had clearly heard the squeaking.

When she returned to Mrs. Meyer dusk was already closing in. "I travelled with Earl Luigi all the way to the sky!" she exclaimed excitedly. "First we went round and round the trunk of the cherry tree up to the highest branch and then across the roof of your house up into the sky!"

"Earl Luigi?" Mrs. Meyer said amused. "Sometimes he is a bit of a fraud, our rusty Rudy."

Before Eli could say anything else she added: "The thing with the train in the garden was Otto's idea and since it was not really waterproof, he called it Rusty Rudy. And later the nettles grew over it." She smiled to herself. Eli had the feeling that Mrs. Meyer had totally forgotten that she was there. "My Otto really was a nutty chap." She looked at Eli. "If you like, we can make a soup out of it next year. In autumn it doesn't taste as nice."

"You want to make soup out of Luigi?" Eli asked indignantly.

Mrs. Meyer laughed. "No, the nettles of course. In spring the fresh sprigs taste really delicious. But of course your grandma told you all about that too, didn't she?"

Eli nodded. "So what is Earl Luigi's name: Rudy or just Luigi or what?"

"Well, what's your name?" Mrs. Meyer asked amused. "Elisabetha? Ronia? Or just Eli?"

"If you're telling me the truth, then he lied to me about his aristocratic name!"

"It is a pretty story. Who knows whether it's true or not?"

That was not the kind of answer that helped Eli. One of the two had told a fib and she had to find out which one.

Although dusk was already closing in, she would not let anyone stop her from going back to the pond. If what Mrs. Meyer had said was the truth, Rudy was not Luigi and did not live in a mysterious root but beneath some boring nettles. On the other hand: she had travelled with him. She could not have been fooled, or could she? There was only moss on the stump now, nothing else, no matter how Eli searched and called. Maybe he had gone to sleep by now and did not hear her? Or maybe it was because of the fading light that she could not find him anywhere? Eli ran around the pond to the far bank. The grass reached up to her knees; bushes and shrubs intermingled with autumn asters, colours fading in the dusk and sundry clumps of nettles.

She tripped over something. Eli pushed the grass aside with her shoe and saw the remains of an old rotten tree stump. And there it was: a toy train complete with coal tender and a red rusty carriage. But it was a lot larger than Luigi! Eli flinched, stung by the nettles. So there was a train after all. But no matter how much she talked to

it, it answered to neither Rudy nor Luigi. Something rustled near the pond and a shadow scurried under the root stump.

A slowworm? Or was it ...? Eli returned to the terrace contemplating the situation. "I don't understand it. I talked to him and we travelled through the garden. And he was tiny and said he was a magnificent ship."

Mrs. Meyer's wrinkles crinkled on her forehead with amusement. "For my Otto it was Rudy the rusty train, for you it's Luigi the funny locomotive."

"That doesn't make sense!" Eli said.

"Why?" the old lady asked, sounding genuinely surprised.

Only when Eli arrived home did she realise that she had not told Mrs. Meyer about a funny locomotive. She had not mentioned Grandma Mary's nettle soup either. So how could she know? Had she overheard her by the pond? Or had Eli only dreamed of the funny locomotive! What if what Nick had said were true, that you could hear butterflies: did that apply to thoughts and dreams as well? Eli reflected. She had only told Mrs. Meyer about her grandma, but had not mentioned her name. Okay, she could not have meant Grandma Augusta who did not even know that nettles were called nettles. And what if Mrs. Meyer had known Grandma Mary? Maybe from the times when Grandma Mary had still been married to grandpa Friedhelm and had still had that beautiful cherry tree garden? Maybe that garden was even somewhere nearby? No, Grandma Mary had said that it was far away from here. And Pa had said so too. But Mrs. Meyer had known that Eli's name was Elisabetha – and Ronia, even though it was her and Pa's big secret. There was only one explanation: Mrs. Meyer must know Pa!

Eli opened the window. The street lamps scattered yellow patches of light onto the pavement and a thin moon was in the sky. If Pa knew Mrs. Meyer he would have told Eli. Surely he would! And even more surely he would never have given away one of their big secrets! Anyway, Mrs. Meyer lived too far away from Pa. And why would he have told her about Grandma Mary's nettle soup which he had never liked? No, that could not be true. Eli agonised and brooded. Had she mentioned it herself after all? Maybe at some point she had in-

advertently blurted it out during their daily mint tea-time on Mrs. Meyer's terrace without even realising it? The more Eli tried to remember, the less she succeeded. Her thoughts twirled round and round like a roundabout until she was thoroughly dizzy.

Suddenly, she had to laugh. Did any of this matter at all?

She closed the window and went to sleep.

Winter.

A man who does not think for himself
does not think at all.

Oscar Wilde

CHAPTER FOUR

Even after all the leaves had fallen, the old garden remained hidden. Eli leaned far out over the railing on Emma's balcony, but could still only make out some weathered roof tiles between the naked cherry tree branches, the rusty weather cock on the pavilion and a dark shimmering corner of the pond. And a forest of bamboo behind the part of wall that bordered the terraced house garden of Emma's parents. Eli liked the bamboo because it was so big and green and for its rustling leaves that told stories of a far away, foreign country.

Emma's mother did not like the bamboo because it was forever dropping its leaves over the wall onto their grass and she also objected to the shadow it cast. And since her mother did not like it and as she always disliked whatever her mummy disliked, Emma did not like it either

Eli would have loved to give her a good shake. How could anyone be so terribly good and boring at the same time? Maybe it was because of her father? Eli had not met him yet, but a Pa who could not tell stories was surely one of the most tedious in the world. Emma had mentioned that he never read to her! Although this was difficult to believe, since Emma almost always told the truth, it was probably true. She did not call him Pa either, but daddy. Mummy and daddy – only little children used those names! Naturally, Emma knew nothing of the adventures of Ronia, but when Eli offered to tell her she just waved her off.

"Why should I even think about some made-up story? I prefer thinking about real things such as how to begin my essay on my favourite adventure."

That she was not sure how to start did not come as a surprise, Eli could well understand this: but how could someone like Emma have a

favourite adventure at all? "You honestly can't imagine being a fairy, or a troll, or maybe a robber girl? Or at least imagine that you might meet one?"

Emma looked annoyed. "How can you possibly wish to be a robber girl?"

Once again, Eli tried to explain to her about Ronia and Matt's Fort, but Emma interrupted. "My daddy says that robbery is a serious offence and anyone who does anything like that deserves to go to prison for a long time."

Whatever an offence was, Eli did not like it. She was Ronia the robber's daughter: strong, brave, adventurous and wild! And Pa was the unconquerable robber chieftain Matt, whom she loved more than anything as it was he who protected her against dark trolls and rumphobs.

"My daddy catches robbers you know", said Emma. "He even has a real pistol and would shoot them if they don't do exactly as he says." Her cheeks glowed with pride. "My daddy is a policeman."

Eli did not want to admit it, but being a policeman was almost as good as being a robber chieftain.

"And because my daddy is a policeman, I have to obey the law", Emma added almost ceremoniously.

Eli would have loved to run away. It was so unfair! Why did stupid Emma have such an interesting father whilst hers had gone?

This Christmas was the saddest Eli had ever had. In years past, Pa had taken her along for what he called Christmas tree procurement. Always at the last moment, Ma used to say. With his robber-chieftain-smile, Pa used to sweep aside her fear of ending up with the last crooked as a rake tree. He just gave her a peck on her cheek and said he had his special sources. Ma then looked a little cross, but only a little. Pa had journeyed half across town and in a flash found a huge, bolt upright tree and tied it to the roof of car roof overhanging front and back. Then the neighbours had to help lug it up to the flat where Ma threw up her hands in dismay for it was impossible to fit the thing into the living room.

But miraculously, the "thing" did fit, every year, and as soon as the tree was in its stand, Eli had to leave the room and was not allowed

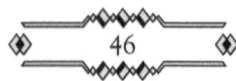

back until later in the evening when Pa rang the little bell. It smelt of gingerbread and candle wax, cracked nuts and the stew they always had for Christmas Eve. The tree was a fairy tale of lights, and baubles, and stars made of glass. And Ma was happy because everything looked so beautiful, and Pa was happy because Ma was happy.

Then they all sang a song together and Eli was happy to finally be allowed to unpack her presents under the tree of lights. And Ma and Pa loved watching her. And then the doorbell rang, and Grandma Mary brought in her home-made chocolate cake, and Grandma Augusta called from somewhere to say she had put a little something into Eli's bank account and that she could not make it this year because of other commitments; but next time she would definitely be there! Everyone laughed because they all knew that Grandma Augusta could not stand Christmas and that she always planned her trips to make sure she was definitely not around.

This year Grandma Augusta called from Tokyo and of course Grandma Mary was not going to be there with her chocolate cake anymore. Eli hoped she would not be looking down from her heavenly garden to see what had become of their festivities. As Ma's living room was small, only a small Christmas tree would fit. And because Pa was not around anymore to buy it and Ma did not have time, she had ordered a box of green plastic bits from a catalogue that were supposedly assembled in "only a few simple steps" to make it a fantastically real-looking Christmas tree. Actually, there were a lot of steps necessary and the result smelled of a mixture of toothpaste and washing powder.

"At least it doesn't shed its needles", Ma said, but she did not look very happy.

Pa came around that evening, saw the tree, but said nothing. He did not look happy either and anyway, nothing was as it should have been on such an evening. Because Eli had already seen the decorated tree, Pa did without the bell this year, and Ma had a headache, and did not want to sing. So the separated sat quietly side by side on the sofa and watched Eli unpack her presents: a yellow anorak and winter boots in red from Ma, a sea-blue bathrobe and two hair clips from Pa. And the plate full of vanilla biscuits was not home-made because Ma

had not had time for it. They ate in the kitchen. The stew came from a tin because Ma had come back late from work and Pa was good at almost everything but cooking. They ate dinner in silence and for the very first time Eli was glad when Pa left. She wished Ma a good night and fled up to her room.

The moon shone through the window. Eli opened it; a small flurry of snow was blown inside. She tried to find the cherry tree in the dark and the longer she looked, the more she was able to make out its silhouette of black branches against the moon and the restless night clouds. What might Mrs. Meyer be up to now? Was she giving Nick and Luigi their presents on the terrace, all alight with candles? Brrrr! It was too cold for that. Might she be sitting in her house, all by herself, crying because no one had come to visit?

Eli looked at the flower lattice. It was rustier than Luigi, but Luigi was funny and the lattice was dull. Eli crept into the living room and put on her new anorak and red boots which were soft and warm.

The world was different in the dark and the gap in the wall led into a mysterious wonderland. The moon transformed trees and bushes into shadowy creatures and threw a pale light across the grey grass. Eli ran over to the cherry tree to wish Nick the season's greetings. His pointed cap had slid over his face; feet, legs and hands were covered in withered leaves. If Eli had not known better, she could have sworn she heard snoring coming from beneath the cap.

This impossible troll was actually managing to sleep through Christmas Eve! But Mrs. Meyer was still awake. At least Eli presumed so from the faint light that shone from the window onto the terrace. She tried to look inside but could not see a thing. A black cloud pushed rudely in front of the moon. Stars twinkled around it. Was Grandma Mary celebrating Christmas in her heavenly garden, too?

"I'm going to take Eli briefly over to mother's to bring back the cake tray", Pa used to say when Ma served the chocolate pudding after the roast goose on Christmas Day. Although Ma nodded kindly, Eli always had the feeling that she somehow disapproved of the visit. You could only fit a very small Christmas tree into Grandma Mary's little house, even smaller than the one Ma had stuck together this year. But it had always looked so beautiful: red and gold angels and

lots of sweets with holes in the middle, so you could thread string though and hang them on the fragrant branches. Grandma Mary gave Pa and Eli hand-knitted mittens and stripy socks, and for Ma it was always home-made garden goodies such as strawberry and gooseberry jam, elderberry syrup, pickled gherkins, jars of sauerkraut and loads of nuts, apples and pears. When they returned home in the evening with all their luxuries, the aroma of crispy duck roast still lingered in the hallway. Ma looked at all the boxes and then at the clock shaking her head, and Pa used to give her a kiss and everything was fine.

Suddenly the terrace door opened.

"Come in", Mrs. Meyer said. That was all. No questions about how, where or why or whatever else grown-ups always wanted to know if children did something unusual.

Eli was surprised to find that Mrs. Meyer's living room looked almost exactly the same as Grandma Mary's. Even the tiled stove had the same grassy green colour. Candles made flickering shadows dance across the walls and the top of the Christmas tree touched the ceiling. There were so many baubles, stars and angels hanging on the tree, one almost had the impression Grandma Mary and Ma had decorated it twice. Only the sweet titbits were missing. Instead, it smelled of vanilla biscuits and sprigs of fir.

Then a little bell tinkled.

Eli just stood there in amazement and Mrs. Meyer said: "Don't you want to unwrap your present?"

"But I don't have one for you", Eli said sadly.

The old lady smiled. "Oh but you have. You are here."

A packet wrapped in blue with a silver bow lay beneath the tree. "What's inside?" Eli asked.

"Maybe it's what you wish for the most?"

Curiously Eli took the packet. It was very light and she just could not imagine what might be inside. For sure, one thing could not be inside: her most important wish. Or maybe it was? She looked at Mrs. Meyer enquiringly; she just shrugged. "Rudy brought it over a while ago. He is out distributing presents. At least that is what my nutty Otto used to say, so I guess it's to be believed."

Eli laughed, fiddled the bow open and removed the paper. Out came a little red box. Eli opened it – and tears of disappointment cascaded down her cheeks.

"Don't you like your present?" Mrs. Meyer asked.

"You fibbed! There's nothing inside!"

"How could I know your most important wish, dear child?"

"But you just pretended you did!"

"No. I said that maybe your most important wish is inside the packet, but not what your most important wish is."

For the first time Eli was cross with the old lady who looked as sweet as Grandma Mary, but seemed now a sly old dog just like Grandma Augusta. "I told you the other day! I want Ma and Pa to love each other again so we can all live in our old flat, and I mean: everything should be just as it was before."

"What do you mean: *before?*" Mrs. Meyer asked kindly.

"When Pa used to tell me stories in the evening, and we visited Grandma Mary at Christmas."

"And when do you think *before* started?"

What a silly question! Eli opened her mouth and closed it again. If she thought about it, it was not so simple: indeed, shortly after Grandma Mary had moved to heaven, Eli had learned to read. And even though she loved Pa's stories more than anything else, it was interesting to finally understand the captions below the colourful pictures in her big book of common knowledge, and what was written on the posters in the shop windows and on mum's tubes and jars in the bathroom. If Grandma Mary were to be back, she would not be able to do any of those things. And if they were back in the old flat, she would be unable to come to Mrs. Meyer's garden because it was too far away. She would have Pa back but instead she would never see Nick, Mrs. Meyer and funny Luigi again; and Emma. Well, she could do without Emma. But it would be even worse: if everything was as before, she would never ever have discovered the old garden! She would not even know it existed. No, that had not been a silly question but a very clever one. And a very complicated one, too.

Mrs. Meyer smiled. "You should look again and see what's really inside the packet."

Eli was sure that there was still nothing inside as before; she had not put it down for a moment. Nevertheless she looked at it again, shook it, turned it around and upside down. Not even a speck of dust fell out. "There, you see! Nothing!"

"Maybe your most important wish was a little too vague", the old lady said and held the box up so Eli could look inside. "Look: there's space for everything that is going to come after yesterday. Tomorrow."

Eli's thoughts turned a somersault and she then understood: she had to start the other way round! She must not wish for things that had been, but wish for things to come and how they should be.

She took the box and ceremonially spoke inside: "I wish that Pa and Ma love each other from tomorrow on, and that the three of us will soon move to Mrs. Meyer's, and that I can spend every day of the new year with Nick and Luigi in the garden, and that I do not have to come and visit secretly anymore." She looked at Mrs. Meyer. "And anyway, I would really like it if we all ate chocolate cake together on Sundays, here on your terrace."

It took quite a while before the old lady answered. "What if your parents wish for something else? And maybe me too?"

"I thought you were happy not to be alone!" Eli replied disappointedly. "Grandma Mary always complained that we did not come over often enough. And that her back hurt, and she could not manage the garden anymore and ..."

"I am only visiting."

"But who are you visiting? No one lives here!"

Mrs. Meyer sat down on the stove bench. "I can't tell you."

"And why not?" Eli shouted. "Were you telling fibs all the time, and this isn't your house after all? And not your garden? And you're secretly creeping in here just as I do?"

The wrinkles around Mrs. Meyer's eyes lined into a mischievous smile. "Well, something of that kind."

She looked like Pa when he had one of his silly ideas. For example, looking for rumphobs near the elephants in the zoo. And when Eli had answered in a grown-up way: "Oh please! There are no rumphobs here!" Pa had said: "And how do you know before having looked

everywhere?" Although he knew exactly that nobody was permitted to look everywhere!

Suddenly it was no longer important to know why the old lady was here; it was just important she stayed.

Eli sat down with her on the warm bench and they watched the flickering candles, ate vanilla biscuits and drank mint tea. And then Eli told the story of Ronia, the robber's daughter. When she had finished, Mrs. Meyer told the story of a little boy-prince who had had only a single flower in his garden because his garden was tiny, but at the same time a complete and whole round world. "And this single beautiful flower was a rose. But as the little prince didn't know this, he had to find out first and so he went on a long, dangerous journey ..."

Here Mrs. Meyer ended. Eli thought that was really cruel, but no matter how much she begged, she could not entice the old lady to continue. "The end is where it finishes", she said. "And we are not there yet."

To Eli, this was as clear as mud, but she had already decided that when Mrs. Meyer said odd things, she would not think about them any further. Grandma Mary had also said odd things sometimes. Pa said that it was her age. And if it had been age with Grandma Mary, then it was definitely the case with Mrs. Meyer; after all, she had been married for sixty-six years!

Eli nibbled the last vanilla biscuit and said goodbye. She desperately wanted to know why Luigi had sent her this peculiar present. As the moon was hiding behind the clouds, it was now pitch dark in the garden. Eli stumbled over to the pond and called out for Luigi. Nothing moved. She sat down by the bank and waited. Slowly the moon pushed away the clouds and the little stream burbled loudly in the night. The black water rippled where it reached the pond, but by the big root it was smooth and glossy and reflected the cold moon. Maybe Luigi was delivering presents somewhere else? No way! That was total nonsense: there was no Father Christmas and it could not therefore be a train that delivered the Christmas presents! Make room for tomorrow, Mrs. Meyer had said. What if tomorrow was as gloomy as the winter sky? How Eli would have loved to pack the sum-

mer sun into the empty box, together with all those beautiful days she had spent with Pa and Ma. And the wonderful smells from the old kitchen, and a few of those creaking planks from the corridor. And Pa's stories on top, the funny ones and the adventurous ones, the exciting ones and the one about the old garden which was a little sad. A new morning, a new day, a new year. Many years. Eli saw Pa and Ma and Grandma Mary and Grandma Augusta, and then she saw herself, but she was not at school any more but was Ma, and then she was Grandma, and Pa was a strange old man with whom she drank coffee. And then she sat on a weathered wooden bench that was built around the old cherry tree. And you could hear children's screams of delight from somewhere and the croaking of a frog. She was in Mrs. Meyer's garden, and then again, she was not. She looked over to the house which somehow looked deserted; no lights any more, nothing. Mrs. Meyer had probably gone to sleep.

Eli dug her fingers into the soft moss, which was black and, just as the water, with silvery sprinkles from the moon. She held onto the earth, crying. She did not feel the biting cold, but could feel the warmth of spring. There was something round, firm ... little bulbs with a pale shimmer. The pale moon shimmered too, and the passing clouds were not black any more, but grey and a little red around the edges. The black moss turned grey and green and the shadowy shapes turned into bushes, trees and grass – it surely was not morning yet?

"Eli? Eli! Are you in there?"

That came straight from the sky. Had the angels come to take her with them? She would be able to fly up and finally visit Grandma Mary in her heavenly garden. Suddenly she understood why Luigi so desperately wanted to be an airship.

"Gosh, get out of there! They're looking for you!"

No, that definitely was not an angel. It was a grey gnome directly from Matt's Wood, with fat Emma's voice, which did not come from the sky, but from the balcony of the house next door. What did she say? Why would somebody be looking for her? Anyway, the silly-billy could not see her from up there! Just let her scream as much as she wants! Eli felt uncomfortable and realised that, despite her new ano-rak, she was terribly cold. Anyway, no one was here anymore so she

might as well leave. "You shouldn't sit on wet grass!" she could hear Ma say and she wished she had listened. Her bottom was soaking wet.

She squeezed through the gap in the hedge, trembling.

"I knew it!" Emma said and brushed the moss and leaves from her jacket as her mother would have done.

Eli was furious. The fearless Ronia would never have let a boring homebody straighten her clothes! She slapped Emma's hands away. "Good children should be in bed fast asleep at this time of the night!"

"But they're looking for you", Emma repeated tearfully. It was only then that Eli noticed that all the houses had their lights on, and people walking about, and police cars with flashing blue lights were in front of their house. What was this all about?

Then she saw Ma- and Pa! They were speaking to a policeman, gesturing manically.

"My daddy", Emma said proudly, but Eli did not hear her any more. She ran across the road, straight into Pa's arms and he squeezed her so hard, she almost could not breathe. Ma cried and Pa took her into his arms. Eli could not remember when she had last been so happy. Her most important wish had come true in the end!

"Please, please don't ever do that again", Pa said.

Eli had no idea what he was talking about. When he carried her into the house, the moon had faded and as the morning dawned, soft snow began to fall.

CHAPTER FIVE

Pa took her to bed and Ma brought up a hot cup of tea. Eli imagined how they both sat squeezed into Luigi's red parcel and had great difficulty fighting back a loud laugh. Where on earth had she left the little box? Pa stroked her hair. "We were dreadfully scared that something had happened to you."

„The police were just about to send for reinforcements to search the overgrown garden!" Ma said. Eli suddenly started to sweat. Surely Emma had snitched on her to her policeman daddy. She would never exchange a single word with this traitress ever again!

"I walked around a bit in the dark", she said. "And then I fell."

"Where was that?" Ma wanted to know.

Eli shrugged. She looked at Pa. "Are you going to read me a good-night-story?"

He smiled. "I bet I know which one you would like to hear?"

Eli spent the last week of the year in bed with fever, a cough and the sniffles, but that did not bother her as long as Pa visited her every day!

On New Year's Eve Ma had to work; Pa wanted to visit them in the evening to celebrate. Eli had promised faithfully to stay in bed. After half the morning had passed, she was bored. Then she had to go to the bathroom which did not really count as getting out of bed, even if it took a little longer, and anyway, someone had to air the room at some point. The air that blew in was icy. It had stopped snowing and the naked branches of the cherry tree looked as mouse-grey as the sky behind. How Eli would have loved to go across to it, but she knew that that would definitely not pass as "staying-in-bed". She closed the window and if she was honest with herself was happy to get back under the warm blanket.

She awoke when the door-bell rang. Maybe Pa had come over early? Ma would not ring the bell. Quickly she got up and slipped into her new bath robe. The ringing turned into a knock. That could only be Pa! Eli ran down the hall and opened the door. Emma was standing there with a plastic bag in her hand.

"Hello", she said shyly. "I've been meaning to visit you for a while, but my mummy wouldn't let me. She said you needed a rest."

Eli would have loved to slam the door in her face. Emma pointed at the bag. "I brought you something."

"Well", Eli said rather indolently. She led the way to her room, got into bed and pulled her blanket up to her chin. "I really shouldn't have visitors you know. And right now I do not feel too well."

Emma sat down on the edge of the bed and looked around. Eli thought of Emma's beautiful room and was embarrassed. "So? What did you bring?"

"I didn't know what you needed it for, but I thought I'd better keep it for you."

Now Eli became curious. "What do I need what for?"

Emma dug out a piggy-pink-coloured sandwich box with Luigi's parcel inside! It was dented and soaked.

"Where did you get that from?" Eli asked puzzled.

"You brought that back from the garden!" When Eli did not answer she added: "And then you dropped it when you saw your daddy and mine. Don't say you don't remember?"

Eli could not even remember taking the box from the house. Why was there wet earth inside it? White bulbs were embedded in the earth, a little moss and a wilted cherry tree leaf. Eli remembered sitting on the banks of the pond, but definitely not recalled anything else.

"You told on me, you snitch!" Eli said angrily.

Emma blushed. "I didn't! My daddy asked if I knew where you might be, but I said I didn't know. Although I could have guessed that you were in the forbidden garden. And that's why I went up to the balcony and called you. Then I went over to the wall and there you were. It's not right for you to go in! And I have to take the box back."

"Really, you didn't tell on me?"

„Definitely not! You're my friend." She sounded so serious and honest that Eli at once regretted her nasty thoughts. Maybe someone could be boring and still be nice? She pushed her blanket aside.

"I'll have a look to see if I can find something to put the bulbs into."

She could not find anything, but then remembered that Grandma Mary had kept her flower seeds in old yoghurt pots. She fetched a strawberry yoghurt from the fridge, shared it with Emma, washed the pot, cut a hole in the bottom with the kitchen scissors and put the earth and bulbs inside. The pot was not big enough, so they ate another yoghurt, cherry, all the while giggling and fooling around. The afternoon flew quickly by.

When Emma had left, Eli put the yoghurt pots outside onto the windowsill. Again, another wish had come true: she had wished to go into the old garden and promptly Emma had visited and brought her a little scent and some earth – and even a leaf from her favourite tree! Carefully Eli straightened Luigi-Rudy's parcel out and put it on the radiator to dry. She wondered what was going to grow from the bulbs.

Ma was tired when she got home. Eli told her about Emma's visit and she said: "That's nice." Eli had the feeling she had not listened and she did not see the yoghurt pots in front of the window either. Pa noticed them immediately.

"Emma gave them to me", Eli said. "Apparently something really great is going to grow from them in springtime."

Pop laughed and Eli felt wicked for not telling the truth. She had never done it in the past. But the past was gone. Mrs. Meyer was right: you could not turn back time, only hope for the future.

On New Year's morning the sun shone brightly into the room. Eli's throat was not scratchy any more, the sniffles were not worth mentioning and she felt altogether great. She jumped out of bed whistling and went to the living room. The sofa, where Pa had slept, was empty. The cushions were lined up neatly the way Ma liked them. From the kitchen she could hear the rattling of the dishes and it smelled of freshly baked bread rolls. Ma had made breakfast – just as she used to! The fact that the sofa was unused surely meant that Pa had slept in Ma's room?

Eli stormed into the kitchen. "I am terribly hungry!"

Ma brewed the coffee. "I'm almost done. You can carry the tray over."

There was butter, milk, jam, honey and Eli's favourite salami, all on the tray. And the dishes: two plates, two cups, two sets of cutlery.

"Your father has already left", Ma said. "And the two of us are going to have a really lovely New Year's breakfast, what do you think?"

The lump in Eli's throat was so large, she was sure she would not be able to eat a single bite.

The January weather matched Eli's mood perfectly. Grey clouds over grey houses, rain, storms. She was sad and furious: with Ma who did not seem to mind that Pa was not there anymore and with Pa who did not have time for her, with Emma who got on her nerves with her chitter-chatter, with Nick who got on her nerves by being quiet and with Luigi who was nowhere to be seen. And she was especially furious with Mrs. Meyer who had lied through her teeth: nothing, absolutely nothing of her most important wish had come true!

Eli stuffed the crumpled little red parcel into the very farthest corner of her desk and decided to never ever go back to the garden again. She then grabbed the two yoghurt pots and threw them into the rubbish. And then she was furious with herself for searching the rubbish for those stupid bulbs, and because there was not enough soil left, and because she kept constantly looking out of the window towards the cherry tree. And because she longed for the garden. Nonsense, she did not long for it! She was just going to go over quickly and fetch a little more earth so the bulbs could grow. But she was not going to talk to Mrs. Meyer. Not a single word. And not to Luigi-Rudy either! Actually, she did not even have to go to the garden!

At the end of the road there was a flower shop where she could ask for some soil. Just let them jolly well see what they were going to do if she stopped coming to visit! Contentedly, she ate a lemon yoghurt, washed the pot and went on her way. The shop was rather small and it seemed to Eli that she was the first person to enter in a long time. Roses, tulips and carnations flowered in grey and green buckets and on a shelf there were colourful pots with miniature plants which Eli

did not recognise; one of the pots was as yellow as the sun with a delicate fern growing inside. When Eli touched it, the leaves quickly folded and it turned into a dried weed. Startled, she pulled back her hand.

"Good afternoon", said a friendly voice from behind. Eli turned around. An elderly lady stood in front of her, not quite as old as Mrs. Meyer because her hair was not white yet. Also, she did not have as many wrinkles on her face. She wore a baggy green cardigan, a washed-out brown pair of trousers and her hands were mottle-stained with soil.

"I really hardly touched it", Eli said contritely.

"Well, it's a mimosa", the woman explained smiling. "Don't worry: it will soon unfurl itself again. What can I do for you?"

Eli held out the yoghurt pot. "I need a little soil. How much would it cost, please?"

The woman laughed. "If that's all, it's free. What do you need it for?"

Eli told her that she had been given bulbs which she wanted to plant and put in front of her window. But she deliberately kept the fact to herself that she did not even know if they were actually bulbs and that she had taken them from Mrs. Meyer's garden. The woman did not ask anything further and disappeared. She returned shortly afterwards with the soil and a little sky-blue flowerpot. "This is lucky clover. People give it to each other on New Year's Day; unfortunately, this one was left over. Would you like to have it?"

It was incredible: there was a real four-leaf clover sprouting from the little pot! "Yes, but – how much is it?"

Again, the woman laughed. "A little present on the house. But please don't put it outside, it will freeze." She wrapped the yoghurt pot into one small bundle and the clover pot between two layers of paper. Eli took the precious packets with an exuberant thank-you. The year just had to be good with all that lucky clover! Even without Mrs. Meyer's old garden.

The soil was just enough and it was good to have the bulbs sitting in front of the window again. But it was even better to look at the little sky-blue pot. The clover leaves had a darker centre which looked

really pretty. Carefully, Eli stroked them and felt a tiny bit of luck tickling her thumb. She thought of the little mimosa that did not like to be touched. How different those plants were!

When Eli woke-up on the last day of her holidays, it had snowed. The roofs were a cloudy white and she could not wait to get down into the street. But what a disappointment it was when she saw the mushy slush on the road and the dirty pavement with the salt crystals from the gritting lorry. There were tracks on the empty piece of barren land, but none of them led to the old wall. Eli ran criss-cross until everything was covered in shoe prints and then she quickly slipped into the garden, forgetting that she had never wanted to go back. On the other side of the wall the paths were powdered white bands, the bushes and the grass had white little caps on and the cherry tree wore white sashes on which the sun had embroidered glittery crystals.

Nick leaned against a trunk and slept. He, too, had a snowy cap and was wrapped into a fluffy white blanket under which his naked toes peeked out. The pond was frozen over and on the ice was a thin dusting of powdered snow. The tree stump glistened like an enchanted mini mountain. However, there was no trace of Luigi, the funny locomotive. As Eli walked towards the house there was not a sound to be heard. Mrs. Meyer was not sitting on the terrace as it was too cold. She sat on the stove bench and there was the delicious aroma of mint tea.

"Lovely to see you", she said. No questions, no accusations.

Eli actually forgot that she was angry with her. "Where is your Christmas tree?"

"Christmas is over, isn't it? Did you find a suitable place for your snowdrop bulbs?"

So they were snowdrops! How did Mrs. Meyer know she had taken the bulbs?

"You have to put them outside. They need the cold."

"But I did! I even got soil from the little corner shop. The flower lady was really very nice and gave it to me for free."

"It is good you went there."

Eli sat beside her on the warm bench. "Why?"

"Because you learned that some things are only beautiful as long as you don't touch them."

This could not be true. It was impossible for Mrs. Meyer to know that she had touched the mimosa fern!

"But the lucky clover reminds you of laughing and being happy."

"You can't possibly know that."

The old lady smiled. "What can't I possibly know? That there are plants which like to be in the shelter of a room or in the shade and others that love the cold, the sun and the wind? That they all need water and a little soil so they can grow and flourish?"

"You can't possibly know that!" Eli insisted. Mrs. Meyer went to the window. There, there were colourful pots with plants that flowered and some that were just green, huddled side by side. Eli tried to re-member if they had been there during her last visit. She did not know.

Mrs. Meyer took a little sunny-yellow pot with a tiny fern and gave it to her. It was the mimosa from the flower shop. "I know because you know."

"Eli! Wake up!"

It took a while until she realised that it was not Sunday, but Mon-day morning and she had to get up because the school holidays were over. And that Ma was in a hurry, and impatient, and nervous, and just as tired as Eli.

Had she really been back into the garden and in Mrs. Meyer's living room? Or had it just been a dream? Eli struggled out of bed. It was pitch dark outside. The mimosa had folded its leaves away alt-hough no one had touched it and from the clover pot peeped a little chimney sweep with a sign on his ladder that wished 'Good Luck!' How did he get there?

"It was really nice of the woman in the flower shop to give you those two plants", Ma said.

"Yes", Eli said. That really had been nice.

Ma moved the mimosa and the clover to one side and opened the window. "What on earth do you plan to do with the yoghurt pots?"

"They are for spring", Eli said.

CHAPTER SIX

Eli baptised the mimosa 'Mimi' and it became her habit to wish the clover and Mimi a good morning after getting up. As long as it was dark, Mimi had her leaves closed and Eli was glad to see that there were other living creatures that preferred to wake up only if the sun was shining outside, just like herself. While Mimi could fold up her delicate fronds swiftly at any time without much effort, the clover only managed to do the same with its four leaves half way. That looked funny and helped Eli to be happy if a day was especially cold and grey.

Whenever Eli looked at the clover, she remembered an outing with Pa the previous summer: for one whole afternoon they had wandered through fields and meadows in search of four-leaf clover. Although Eli had had the feeling she had turned-over each and every blade of grass twice, they had only been able to find three-leafed ones. Ever since that day, she was convinced there was no such thing as a clover with four leaves. And now she owned a whole sky-blue pot full of it!

The next time Pa came to pick her up, she told him about it.

He laughed. "That doesn't count, robber's daughter! Cultured clover isn't a lucky charm, it's cheating."

"But people give it to each other for New Year!"

"That's because they are too lazy to look for real ones", he said, putting on a conspiratorial face. "There's even five-leaf clover around, you know."

"Now you're really telling fibs!"

"Pardon me: is that the way to speak to a fully-fledged robber chieftain?"

"Sure, if you're his daughter!"

"What the heck, then I suppose I will have to prove it to Ronia with the real green-stuff in hand." He smiled. "Next time we're in Matt's Wood."

"Tomorrow?" she asked.

"Tomorrow", he promised. It was a bit like heaven on earth. When Pa took her home, Ma had not yet returned from work, but Eli did not mind. Tomorrow she would have proof that there really was such a thing as five-leaf clover! She switched on the light in her room and threw her jacket onto the bed. As Mimi was surely already asleep, she was going to tell the folded-up cheating clover off! But what was this? The chimney sweep was standing in his pot all by himself. Around him the clover leaves hung limply from the pot although Eli had watered it in the morning. She could not stop the tears welling-up inside her.

"What is it, my dear?" Ma asked coming inside the door.

Eli had not heard her coming. "My lucky clover has wilted!" Ma dried her tears with the sleeve of her jumper. Later she made noodles with lots of tomato sauce, just as she used to, and afterwards Eli was pleasantly full and went to bed without even turning on the light in her room.

The following day she was really looking forward to answering Emma's same eternal question, with the truth for a change: "No, I don't have time to do homework with you. I am meeting my Pa later on!"

Pa came to pick her up in the car and Eli knew immediately that this was the beginning of an adventurous trip with another secret at the end. The biggest secret she shared with Pa was that he not only called her Ronia for fun, but that it really and truly was her name – her official third name! Eli's second name was Clothilde which was even worse than Elisabetha. She was named after Ma's favourite aunt who had unfortunately died a month before Eli's birth. Ma had felt obliged, Pa said. And of course it did not help, that the other children at school kept calling: Hey, Lisa's bed! Or, even worse, Cloth-Hilda. And then she had gone to Matt's Wood with Pa and in the shade of an ancient oak tree, he had told her the secret: without a soul knowing, using magic ink, he had issued a secret certificate in

the name of Ronia and added it to the official papers – just like his Pa, Grandpa Friedhelm, had done at the time. And that was why Pa was actually called Matt, and Eli was Ronia, his reckless daughter. But no one was ever to know, because as soon as that happened, the magic would be broken and the secret documents would crumble to dust. It was a noble feeling to know something that no one else knew. From then on, Eli had only smiled when others teased her and finally they stopped and simply called her Eli.

The two of them did not just keep big secrets, but small ones too, one of which was that someday they would find a four-leaf clover.

"Where are we going?" Eli asked.

"Let me surprise you." Pa smiled, but Eli thought he looked a bit strained. It was as if he were afraid of something. But what could a robber chieftain like him be afraid of? Whilst Eli's thoughts went round like a whirligig in a storm, they left the town and suddenly she knew where they were going: the *"Little Jug"*, a cosy pub where they served super-yummy chips with home-made ketchup. Ma said chips were unhealthy, especially for children; that's why they never had any at home. Pa knew exactly that Eli liked chips even more than noodles with tomato sauce, and that was why sometimes, after a Saturday shopping trip, he took a detour on the way home, and they had a break at the *"Little Jug"*. This was one of their medium-sized secrets. Pa stopped directly in front of the entrance. "Care for a little refreshment, Ronia-Child?"

"A little refreshment?" Eli called indignantly. "I am as hungry as a dark troll and desperately need a huge robber's portion with a lot of power cream!"

Laughing, they went in. They sat down at their favourite table and Pa ordered two extra large portions and a double portion of ketchup. Everything was as always, apart from the waitress: a young woman with freckles and brown, short hair. When she served the chips she said: "Hi Eli. I'm Kate."

How dare this person disturb her secret meeting with Pa? And how did she know her name?

"Please, I would like to eat!" Eli said angrily and inspected her chips. They did not look as yummy as they normally did.

"Can I get you something to drink?" Kate asked cordially. "Maybe a coke?"

Now, that was really the last straw! Drinking coke was part of the chips secret. "No, thank you. Coke is not good for children."

Kate looked at Pa, and Pa looked at Kate and suddenly he did not look Matt-gutsy anymore, but simply very tired. Eli was embarrassed. He had specially taken the time and trouble to surprise her with her favourite food and she behaved – well, like a mimosa! Against her will, she had to smile. She looked at Kate. "I would prefer a small mineral water! And my father would like a large coke." And then, and she did not know if it was her way of making amends, a guilty conscience or the elated thought of Mimi, or all of the above, she added: "Because I have to drink coke secretly."

Pop snorted with laughter, then Kate, then Eli and they laughed so loudly that the other guests started to stare, but the three did not care. Kate brought water, coke and two straws, and the home-made ketchup tasted delicious, and the chips were even tastier than before, and it was heavenly having another food-secret on the list.

After Eli had emptied her plate right down to the last crumb, Pa put on a solemn face and pulled a white envelope from his pocket. He lowered his voice to a whisper. "Here it is, the promised evidence, dearest daughter."

Excitedly, Eli opened the envelope. Inside a piece of folded paper was a parchment bag with two clover leaves shimmering through. One had four and the other one actually had five leaves! Eli was flabbergasted. "Where did you get those from?"

Pop smiled mischievously. "They grew in a magic clearing, lit by the moon in the middle of Matt's Wood, dearest Ronia, and it was terribly hard work finding them."

Eli laughed, and while she enjoyed chocolate ice cream for pudding and Pa had a coffee, she kept glancing over to the parchment-wrapped treasure. She told Pa about her wilting lucky clover.

He shrugged. "I told you: pseudo-clover just doesn't do."

Eli did not know what pseudo-clover was, but it sounded like something bad, and it was, wasn't it? How was lucky clover supposed to be lucky if everyone could buy it in a shop without any effort? And

on top of that, one that had been left over because no one wanted it? She imagined how Pa had been out night after night since the previous summer until he had found those precious leaves in the moonlight, how he gently picked them and placed them between two pages of a book, just as gently, to dry. All this, just for her! "How long have you had them?" she asked. "And why didn't you tell me earlier?"

"I waited until you needed them."

Eli jumped up and planted a big kiss on his cheek. "You're the best Pa in the whole world!"

When they got back home, she took Ronia's book from the shelf, opened it at the passage where Ronia was reunited with her father and put the parchment bag between the pages. Then she took the sky-blue pot from the windowsill and tipped its contents into the rubbish, including the little chimney sweep.

She hesitated: bulbs once again! Just they were not white this time, but brown and the limp cheat-stalks were still attached. Eli was tempted to close the rubbish bin lid, but curiosity got the better of her. Something was not right here: clover grew from roots! Pa had shown her. She started fishing everything out, emptied a strawberry yoghurt, washed out the pot and put the bulbs in together with the wilted attachment.

She took it to Mrs. Meyer the next day. Wood crackled in the stove and it smelled of roasted chestnuts, just as it had done at Grandma Mary's. Suddenly, Eli wished that Mrs. Meyer was Grandma Mary. There were little bowls of dried flower husks on the living room table - and empty yoghurt pots! It was a little unnerving to see that Mrs. Meyer occupied herself with empty yoghurt pots, too.

"What are you going to use those for?"

The old lady smiled. "I'm looking forward to the new gardening year."

Eli looked at the dried blossoms. "They look really ugly." Mrs. Meyer tore one of the husks apart and out came little black sticks with light beige edges.

"Remember the bed in front of the terrace?"

Eli thought for a moment. Yes, in autumn it had flowered especially colourfully until the frost came. She thought a little more and then the orange, red and yellow flame-like flowers appeared before her inner eye, almost as though they grew right in the middle of the room. She could remember the smell, too: a mixture of resin and wood with a little orange juice. "Marigolds", Mrs. Meyer said. She put the husk with the little sticks into Eli's hand. "Those are their seeds."

"Those sunny-yellow ones?" Eli asked, because she had liked those best.

"I don't know."

"Why didn't you put each colour into a different pot when you collected them?"

The old lady smiled. "Well, you could believe that from a red flower comes a red one and from a yellow one comes a yellow flower. But marigolds change their colours every year." She picked the little sticks from the husks and sorted them into a yoghurt pot. "They don't want to be tamed, that's why I like them."

Eli helped to pick them. "It's a pity that the garden is so dull and sad and nothing grows or flowers in winter."

"Nonsense," said Mrs. Meyer. "Flowers also bloom in winter. You can even harvest things."

"You're telling fibs!" Eli said.

"Well, put your anorak on and come with me."

Outside it was icy and grey. Not really inviting weather to go for a walk, but Mrs. Meyer did not seem to care. They walked past the cherry tree into the front garden.

Leaning against the wall was a pergola which Eli had not noticed before. Cream-white flowers that looked like finest porcelain gleamed in front of it, and above them were rods strewn with sunny-yellow stars interwoven with the wooden lattice.

"Christmas roses and winter jasmine", Mrs. Meyer said. "And this – ", she pointed to a little bush with odd light-yellow strands, "is witch hazel. Smell it!"

The strands were like crinkled threads and smelled deliciously of honey and cream, whetting Eli's appetite. As if she had guessed her

thoughts, Mrs. Meyer said: "And now we're going to harvest." She fetched a spade and a little wooden box from the pavilion and directed Eli to the back garden.

Not far from the mint leaves bed some broken giant stalks were sticking out of the ground. Mrs. Meyer dug up a few and pulled out some knobbly lumps with which she filled the box. It started snowing, and Eli was glad to get back to the house. While Mrs. Meyer washed the lumps, Eli made herself comfortable on the stove bench.

"This is Jerusalem artichoke", the old lady explained and gave her a little golden yellow lump. "A type of sunflower with edible roots. They taste a bit like nuts and are delicious."

Hesitantly, Eli tried, and immediately ate up the whole lump. Ronia could definitely survive on those in case Matt's Fort got snowed in!

Mrs. Meyer put more wood on the fire. "Of course you are right: in winter it's very uncomfortable outside most of the time." She tapped her forehead. "But if the garden outside is asleep, I still have my garden in here. When I'm in my inside-garden I dream of the outside-garden, and what it's soon going to look like again, and what I'm going to plant where, what I want to change, and what I want to keep. My inside-garden is pure pleasure: I can enjoy the smell of spring, the colours of summer, and the abundance of autumn without even lifting a finger. I don't even need to sow, water or weed and still the most beautiful flowers bloom in it."

"Thoughts aren't reality", Eli said.

"Stories aren't reality either", Mrs. Meyer replied. "And we love them anyway."

Eli thought of Ronia and of the girl from the old garden. And of the boy with the rose. "When are you going to finish telling me the story of the little boy-prince?"

"When the time is right."

Suddenly, Eli remembered that she had seen the black and beige marigold seeds at Grandma Mary's. Just like Mrs. Meyer, she had told her about the cheeky flowers that mixed their play of colours anew every year. Maybe thoughts were the truth after all? Mrs. Meyer brought oven-warm bread, butter, cherry jam and a pot of lovely smelling mint tea.

"I had the feeling you were hungry." Eli nodded.

She spread some butter and lots of jam on a slice of bread and bit into it. It tasted of summer. "You are right", she said whilst chewing. "Winter is a time to enjoy your garden, too."

Mrs. Meyer's wrinkles smiled. Curiously, she looked into Eli's yoghurt pot. "What pretty things have you brought?"

Eli took another slice of bread. "My lucky clover has had it. But it doesn't really matter. My Pa gave me a real Matt's Wood magic clover, so I don't need this pseudo stuff anymore."

"So why did you bring it, if you don't care about it?"

"Because there are bulbs and I wanted to ask you why. A something proper lucky clover should not have, and it doesn't grow in the flower shop, but in the meadows, and is really rare and precious!"

"Well, well", Mrs. Meyer said. "What do you intend to do with it once I have answered your questions?"

"Throw it away I suppose. It's of no use anymore."

"How do you know?"

"You can tell!"

"It gave you pleasure for a while." It sounded like the "didn't it?" was missing at the end.

"I didn't know any better at the time!"

"And what do you know now?"

"Lucky clover is green and doesn't have a brown centre like this one. Every leaf a lucky clover: and that's cheating! Anyway, everyone can buy one of those."

"So you're saying the plant is worth nothing because there are so many of them? Before you had to go all the way to Mexico to get it and it was a long and dangerous journey. Mexico is its home land, and indeed, it has nothing to do with the real clover. A few of his relatives live here, too, forest clover for example which..."

"... tastes so sour, it closes the holes in your socks! But of course it has to because otherwise it is ineffective and ..." Eli put her hand over her mouth in shock. By the fraction of an inch she had almost told her biggest secret, how she and Pa had fought against the dark people and had survived only with the help of the magic sour leaves! She hesitated. "Does that mean I can eat those cheat clover leaves?"

"Of course, if they don't happen to be wilted. The real one, the red meadow clover survives with its roots if it is very cold. They can reach down almost two metres into the soil. And the white clover, which you probably know as well, can crawl with its stalks and produce new roots from them. Your lucky clover, however, only grows from these little brown lumps that look like bulbs and that's where it returns after it has flowered."

"It didn't flower!" Eli said indignantly, feeling almost as though the wilted plant had disgracefully betrayed her.

"It is, of course, the wrong time of the year. Only because it looks like clover and has four leaves, people put it in soil in the autumn so it grows at New Year's Eve. It wouldn't do so on its own." Mrs. Meyer took a big book from a shelf and started browsing. "Here, look!" The little pink flowers seemed to hover over the four-leaved leaves. Underneath was the name of the clover which wasn't a clover: *Oxalis Deppei*. Eli snorted with laughter.

"I own an edible ox!"

Mrs. Meyer closed the book. "Isn't it sad that a plant has to die just because we don't understand its need for rest?"

"Rest? What rest?"

"Didn't Nick tell you what a clever gardener does?"

Eli laughed. "Only the necessary. And he has lots of time for waiting."

"And he has to remember the necessary at the right time", Mrs. Meyer added. She put the book back. "For your lucky clover it means: give it darkness, let it dry out, forget about it. But remember to return it to the light at the right time."

Spring.

The highest goal that man can achieve
is amazement.

Johann Wolfgang v. Goethe

CHAPTER SEVEN

Eli had covered her ox plant with a little soil, wrapped it in newspaper together with the pot, and put it into the furthest corner of her night table. But leaving it alone and forgetting it was more difficult than she had thought, especially because there was nothing interesting to discover in the garden. Mrs. Meyer could not even harvest Jerusalem artichoke because everything was frozen stiff. Oh, how she longed for spring!

Once a week, Pa picked her up from school and they drove to the "*Little Jug*" to have chips. It could have been heavenly, if it had not been for stupid Kate. To Eli, she almost seemed to be waiting for the moment Pa came in. She was constantly trying to talk to Eli, but Eli wanted to talk to her Pa and no one else. Finally, Eli said she did not like chips any more, although it was not true. Instead, she suggested going to see the elephants.

During their second visit to the zoo, they bumped into Kate. She said it was her day off, and did Eli and Pa mind if she joined them? Without even looking at Eli, Pa replied *But no of course not!* and what a pleasant coincidence it was, and that he was happy to see her.

Eli was not happy at all. It was a terrible day, and that did not even change when Pa treated her to chocolate ice cream with whipped cream on top. At least the sky shared her frosty mood, it started snowing on the way back. "Don't you like Kate at all?" Pa asked when he stopped at the driveway.

"No!"

Before he could say anything else, Eli got out and ran towards the house. She did not have the slightest desire to share her precious Pa time with anyone else. Even if it were the Emperor of China! She got herself some yoghurt from the kitchen and went to her room. She sat

at her desk and turned on the cassette player. It remained silent and she remembered that it was broken. "You could ask your father to get you a new one for your birthday!" Ma had said irritably.

Snowflakes were getting caught in the lattice in front of her window, and Eli watched how the rust grew a white cap. After a while, the little green tips peeking from the yoghurt pots were covered in snow. Since Eli knew they were snowdrops, she desperately waited for them to flower. In Grandma Mary's garden, the snowdrops had flowered every year, and masses of yellow and purple crocuses. She stroked Mimi's leaves with her fingertips and giggled when they closed up in the blink of an eye.

The tears of the night rain had cried the winter away, it cleared up by morning and in the afternoon the sun shone. Eli hurried to get home, by now finding it convenient that Ma often worked long hours as this enabled her to go to the forbidden garden without lying.

The only disturbance was Emma who stuck to Eli's heels like worn out chewing gum. She might be nice sometimes, but most of the time she bored Eli with her tedious Barbie dolls, and her even more tedious maths puzzles, and her praise for her oh-so-wonderful policeman daddy.

When tennis lessons were not enough to keep her at bay, Eli added therapy. She had heard Ma and Bridget talk about it as if it was some kind of disorder of fantasy, and somehow abnormal, whose fault it might be and if one could do something about it. Whose fault it should be, Eli did not understand, but individual sessions and group discussions sounded almost as good as tennis with a coach. And so Eli went to therapy once a week. Emma immediately told her mummy and since then, surprisingly, she was much nicer to Eli, which was quite pleasant for a change. Sometimes Eli felt a little bad because it was so easy to lie to Emma – but only a little. Anyway, it was Emma's own fault!

If Eli could not go into the garden, she spent her afternoons in the little flower shop at the end of the road, for three reasons. The first one was the flower lady who patiently answered all her questions and never said strange things; the second was that Eli had an explanation for soiled hands and stained trousers when she got home and the

third and most important: Emma could not stand the shop or the flower lady.

And then came the day: one morning five little white flower heads peeked from the yoghurt pots and Eli danced around her room with excitement. Now it would not be long until spring came! After school, there was an extra tennis lesson for Emma and Eli couldn't wait to get back to the garden. Her heart was still pounding when she slipped through the gap in the wall, but she did not feel bad any more: what was so bad if you were keeping an old lady company?

Behind the wall it looked as if the snow had turned into little white flower bells: the pond was lined with a white carpet, Nick slept under the cherry tree on a white bed, and hundreds of them flowered in front of the pavilion together with purple crocuses. Everywhere the winter aconites speckled their sunny yellow in-between. It was wonderful to be back in the outside garden again!

Mrs. Meyer sat in her rocking chair on the terrace, wrapped up in a check blanket and a thick jacket. "Guess what: my snowdrops are flowering as well!" Eli greeted her.

"That's wonderful", the old lady said.

Eli beamed. "Yes, because it's the right time for telling the snow-drop spring story!"

"Well, now I'm curious." Mrs. Meyer lifted the blanket and Eli slipped under it. And then she told the story Grandma Mary had told her every year, as soon as the first snowdrops started flowering in her garden, and sometimes that had been in the middle of winter. She said that, in the beginning of the world, there had been a little bell flower which was very sad because God had no colour left for it. And how it became sadder and sadder because none of the other flowers in the big meadow were prepared to spare a little of their colour, and how it had finally got its colour from the snow. As Eli told her story, the sun broke through the clouds and the snowdrops in the garden started glistening, and it was not Mrs. Meyer any more who listened, but Grandma Mary. And then she told a story and Eli listened, the sun warmed her face, the trees wrapped themselves in bright green, and the wind carried the scent of cowslips towards them.

"You miss your Grandma a lot, don't you?" Mrs. Meyer asked.

Eli nodded. "She said that garden work was a grind, but she loved it although she didn't really have to do it. Pa had told her that she could move into a flat, but she didn't want to. As stubborn as a Prussian donkey, Pa said. But I honestly don't know what a stubborn Prussian donkey is."

"Maybe it needs a little more exercise than other donkeys", Mrs. Meyer said. "Maybe it's called that, so everyone thinks that it needs a little more exercise than others."

That sounded funny. Eli laughed. "If one of my grans needs exercise, that's surely Grandma Augusta. She has travelled around the world at least three times!"

"And, would you like to do that too?"

Eli shook her head. "Grandma Mary was really strict and grumbled if I didn't clean my shoes properly, or didn't empty my plate, but I still preferred to visit her than Grandma Augusta. In winter we sat on the stove bench together, and she made jam just as delicious as yours. And she had mint in her garden, but it didn't grow near a wall, but beside the strawberry bed."

"I know", Mrs. Meyer said.

Eli wondered how on earth she could have known that. But why waste time thinking about it?

"Grandma Mary always said that the old times were better. And Grandma Augusta said that Grandma Mary had no idea because she still lived in her narrow-minded little world. Well, okay, her house was really small and so was her garden, but I never understood. By the way: how big is your garden?"

"You mean this garden here?" It was one of those odd Mrs.-Meyer-questions again.

"Yes, which one did you think I meant?"

"What do you think, how big is it?"

"That's why I'm asking you!"

"Only you can answer that question."

"Why?"

Mrs. Meyer smiled. "Because I believe that it is as big as you imagine it to be."

Oh dear, this was complicated! "You are telling me to wish for a tiny or a huge garden, and it will be that way in reality?"

"No. Take your time and see how many paths there are. Be wise and select one that suits you and be brave to walk it to the very end. Or be even cleverer and turn around if you realise you have taken a wrong turning."

Ronia was clever and Ronia was brave, and she had the whole afternoon! Eli pushed back the blanket. "I can easily do that. But you already know all the paths: can't you recommend one for me?"

"We can walk together for a bit, but I cannot accompany you everywhere."

Eli accepted that. If one had been married for sixty-six years, maybe one was not too steady on one's feet anymore. Maybe Mrs. Meyer did not want to admit that she did not know herself, how big the garden really was? Maybe because she lived here illegally? But Emma had said that the house and garden belonged to her! At least Eli did not believe her when she said she was only visiting. She had never seen another soul anywhere and Nick and Luigi-Rudy could not be considered hosts. Or could they? Anyway, she must have been coming to the garden for quite a while because she had collected marigold seeds and made cherry jam. Or was it all a lie? Maybe she wasn't Mrs. Meyer after all? But who was she? And then: what was she doing here? There were definitely too many complicated questions at the same time and Eli decided that the most sensible thing to do was to get started.

She went over to Nick who dozed amongst the snowdrops. "Do you know how large this garden is?"

The troll did not consider the question to be particularly important because he only opened one eye when he answered: "Up to the bamboo over there."

"That can't be right", Eli objected. "There is the pavilion behind the bamboo."

"Then, why do you ask me if you know already?"

"But I don't know!"

"Why do you want to know?"

"Because it's important."

"And why is it important?"

"Because!" That sounded just like Ma.

Nick lifted the second eye lid. "Look at the tuft of grass over there."

Eli was getting impatient. "Please, what does the tuft of grass have to do with the size of the garden?"

"In front of it, the winter aconite is wilting. Right beside it the daisies are going to flower soon, the rosette is already out. If you look very carefully, you can see the beginning of a bud. And then the ferns will come, and the ants will crawl on them and in summer, the grass is going to flower, and in winter snow will fall on everything." He winked at her. "So, what is it: a big or a small world?"

"You're not taking me seriously!" Eli said annoyed and walked across to the pond. She squatted down by the tree stump. "Hello, Rudy – are you there?"

From the depth of the roots came an indignant: "There is no Rudy here!"

"Er, I meant to say Rudolphius or something, I mean: Luigi, precious ship – can you help me?" Eli heard a grumbling and to her delight she saw the little locomotive with its tender and carriage chugging across the moss. "Where were you during the winter?"

"Frozen. Buried under masses of snow!"

"By the way, thank you for your Christmas present."

"I didn't pick it. Only delivered it."

It almost seemed that the little train was blushing with embarrassment under its rust, but of course that was total nonsense.

"Have you lived here long?"

"As long as I can remember."

"Can you tell me how big the garden is?"

"Of course I can."

"And?" Eli asked excitedly.

Luigi made a little noise which probably was supposed to be a toot, and a tiny cloud came out of his miniature funnel. "Well, what do you know: I can make smoke again! There were still plenty of coal-crumbs in the cinder from the oven that Mrs. Meyer threw onto the compost."

"That's nice", Eli said. "But I had asked you about the size of the garden."

"All the way up to the sky." It sounded as though he really believed it.

"That's not an answer!"

"Why?"

"Because I need to know where it starts and where it ends."

"Of course it starts here." Luigi let off a second little cloud which hovered above the water for a moment before gently rising until it was lost in the pre-spring sky.

"But it might just as well start by the pavilion or at Mrs. Meyer's terrace."

"Why are you asking if you know already?"

"But I don't know!" Eli cried.

"And why do you want to know?"

"Because I'm interested." Eli was gradually starting to get angry. Had Nick and Luigi conspired against her? Or was Mrs. Meyer behind it all? "A garden can never ever stretch all the way up to the sky!"

Luigi proudly let off another cloud. "It can."

"No!"

"Why not?"

Eli suddenly felt very grown up. "Because it's nonsense."

She rose and pulled back her shoulders. What did Ronia need a sleepy troll and a rusty train for anyway? She would find the answer on her own! Resolutely, she walked across the moss, past the pavilion and squeezed through the shrubbery behind it. There was the wall! If she followed it round, she would surely return back here at some point. She just had to count her steps and the mystery would be solved.

After a few metres the jumble of thorns became so dense that she could only guess the wall was still there, but Ronia would not give up just yet! In the pavilion she found old, but still functioning hedge clippers, and she returned cheerfully to the place from which she had come. But was this really the same place? Did the shrubs not look somehow different? And the winter aconites had not been there before. Maybe she just had not noticed them because she had been busy dealing with the thorns? But you could not miss this kind of

yellow! Or could you? So what, it had to be here! For sure. Quite sure. Probably.

Resolutely, Eli cut into the thorns, tore off branches, squashed the aconites until she eventually succeeded. With the clippers in hand, she followed the wall and gave a triumphant: "I knew it!" when she finally reached the opening through which she used to come into the garden. She progressed through the stalks of the Jerusalem artichokes. In order to stay close to the wall, she had to walk across the mint bed and all kinds of greenery that grew in the protection of the old boundary, and over the population of snowdrops that flowered in front of the wall. For a brief moment, she thought she could feel the sadness of the squashed little bells which would no longer ring in springtime. But it was not her fault that the path led her this way!

Anyway: there were so many snowdrops around it did not really matter if a few went missing – or did it? And besides, she had to concentrate on counting her steps. This was more important than worrying about a few bent flowers. She reached the pergola with the Christmas roses whose petals had already changed from white to a light green, then on over to the bamboo until finally the pavilion appeared. She had made it!

Contentedly, she returned to Mrs. Meyer. "Now I know."

"Well, well."

That was not what Eli had wanted to hear. "I know now how many steps it takes!"

"You discovered the right way?"

"Yes! I walked along the garden wall very closely and counted all my steps." She proudly presented her figures. Surely, now Mrs. Meyer would be full of praise! After all, it had taken great effort: not once had she miscounted, even though she did not like maths. She had scratched herself all over and had a blister on her thumb from cutting with the clippers, and she had even stained her new anorak.

"So you know the length of the wall", Mrs. Meyer said. "But if you really want to know the size of the garden, then you have to choose a different path. And rest in between."

"Yes, yes", Eli waved her remark aside. "So I don't miss the daisies amongst the tufts of grass." She was still hoping for the well-earned praise she felt she deserved.

Mrs. Meyer smiled. "Did you know that every snowdrop has a little crown beneath its white covering leaves and that there are hundreds of different green and even yellow patterns on them? Some are striped, some dotted and some are even shaped like a heart or a horse shoe. Of course, you would only notice if you get in close to them; if you bend down and take the trouble to look carefully inside."

Eli was so ashamed, she broke into a cold sweat. "But I wanted to know where the garden ended, I didn't have a choice. I had to walk along as closely as possible to the wall!"

"I thought you were looking for the size, not the boundaries? Anyway, the wall can be seen much better from outside."

Eli realised this was true. She had gone to all the trouble for nothing and to make matters worse, she had trampled over all those poor snowdrops!

Mrs. Meyer got up and folded her blanket away. "Come on, I have something to show you." They went over to the pond. "Look into the water", she bade Eli. "And tell me what you see."

"Water", Eli said.

"And what else?"

"Spiders crawling over the water!" Fascinated, Eli watched as curious insects walked across the shiny surface as if it were a rubber mat.

In the shallow water between the stones, someone had emptied out a whole bucket full of translucent jelly which, on closer inspection, turned out to be numerous little slimy balls, each with a tiny black dot in the centre.

"Water skaters and frog spawn", Mrs. Meyer explained.

"All those dots turn into frogs?" Eli asked amazed.

"First, they turn into tadpoles; dragonfly larvae's favourite dish. There –", Mrs. Meyer exclaimed and pointed towards a large insect which swam swiftly through the water and disappeared under Luigi's root stump. The longer Eli looked, the more the pond seemed to come alive. There were rotund beetles that paddled on their backs, orange dots that seemed to float in the water and strings of algae

woven into green carpets. And the stones by the banks were not just brown and grey as one might think at first glance, they had red and yellow speckles, and moss coloured clouds on them, and the water reflected the bare trees and sky above.

A garden that went all the way up into the clouds. Clouds that came into the garden. What difference did it make?

"Luigi is right", Eli said. "Somehow."

Mrs. Meyer smiled. "And you are too. In a way."

CHAPTER EIGHT

When Eli returned home, Ma was sitting in the living room leafing through some documents. She looked solemn. "Come, sit with me, Elisabetha." It usually meant bad news when she began conversation in that way. Eli hesitantly took a seat on the sofa.

"Your father and I were thinking ..."

"Pa was here?" Eli shouted.

"Yes. And we believe that you ... Well, that you should talk to someone about all that has happened."

About all of what? And who was Someone? Ma enthused about a really nice lady doctor, not far from Pa's flat and that Pa had also promised to take Eli there and pick her up again afterwards. Finally, she understood that they both wanted her to go to have therapy. Eli struggled to suppress a snort of indignant laughter.

"Yes, I'll go if you like."

Ma looked as if the whole of Matt's Fort had been taken off her mind. She took Eli's hand and squeezed it. "You know, we don't want you to suffer from that whole separation thing."

Eli wanted to say: "Then don't separate!" but she suspected that that would not be such a good idea. So she nodded and contemplated that the real going-to-therapy thing would afford two advantages. One was that she had another real excuse to get rid of Emma and the second was the fact she would see Pa more often!

The first appointment was the day after next. Pa arrived on time, but he did not look as Eli remembered him. For the first time she sensed that he might feel her a bit of a nuisance. "Well, what am I supposed to be doing at the doctor's?" she asked on the way to town.

"She's going to talk to you", he replied.

"About what?"

"About the thing with Ma and myself ... It's probably not that easy for you."

"But I don't want to talk about it with a strange woman!"

"She is really nice. You will like her."

Eli thought of Ma and didn't answer.

The day actually turned out to be quite pleasant; the lady doctor wore a bright red pair of glasses and had a mole on her nose. Even though Eli had bombarded her with questions, she had remained really nice. Eli told her about school and about her room, and that Ma had to work a lot, but nothing about the garden or Mrs. Meyer. And, even less would she say anything about Nick and Luigi. The old garden was her secret and hers alone.

On the way back, Pa showered her with questions and Eli tried to work out why she had to go to therapy when she could just as well have told Pa everything. Before she climbed out he gave her a colour-ful piece of string with a key attached.

"So you can get into my flat – just in case I'm not there to pick you up on time someday", he said and Eli was proud because it made her feel really grown-up.

Of course, Eli was not surprised to hear that Mrs. Meyer already knew what she had been up to in town. The more important thing was that the old lady was there at all. And if she insisted on con-tinuing to talk in riddles, Eli could always go and visit the flower lady.

Eli liked going into the little shop almost as much as she liked go-ing to the forbidden garden, especially if it was cold and rainy. There was a table in a side room where the flower lady tied bouquets and conjured-up flower arrangements. Eli loved watching how beautiful works of art were created from leaves and flowers, ferns and fruits. The whole room smelt of leaves and forest, and on the floor there were little heaps of chopped-off stalks and twigs, and velvety green cushions of moss lining a wicker basket.

She definitely had to tell Luigi! Maybe the little train felt like chuf-fing around the shop instead of up into the clouds? What would the flower lady say if suddenly little white clouds started to rise from her moss basket?

"Why do people come in here so rarely?" Eli asked.

The flower lady was putting roses into a bucket of water. "Some of them don't have the money for flowers; others go into town for more choice." For Eli, the world's most wonderful selection was in this shop.

"When I'm grown up and earn my own money, I will buy a bouquet of flowers from you every day. I promise!"

The flower lady smiled.

"Don't you believe me?" Eli asked in a bit of huff.

"Yes, yes of course I do!" She then pointed to a heap of stalks and twigs. "Will you help me carry those out?"

Eli nodded. Even though she really liked the flower lady, she had never mentioned that Mrs. Meyer was still alive. The lady was only aware that Eli knew of the forbidden garden; but that was not really surprising as she lived immediately opposite. More surprising was the fact that, despite them not looking at all alike, Eli kept mixing-up the flower lady and Mrs. Meyer.

"Why don't you have flowers as pretty as those of the flower lady?" Eli enquired on her next visit. Mrs. Meyer's wrinkles smiled.

"Because, in my outside garden, the time isn't right for them yet."

"And when is the right time?"

The old lady shrugged. "No one will be here to plant and water them."

"You are here."

"I'm only visiting."

"And that's a lie!" Eli blurted out.

The wrinkles stopped smiling. "Unfortunately it isn't."

"Unfortunately? Why unfortunately? Tell me, who are you visiting!"

"Why?"

"Because I want to know."

"Why?"

"Because I have known for a long time that this garden is actually yours!"

"And how do you presume to know that?"

"From Emma."

"So, and what else does your friend tell you?"

"She is not my friend."

"Why not?"

"Because she's daft. Because she says that you are ... Because she tells lies!"

"So it isn't my garden then?"

Eli's eyes filled with tears. "You can be very mean you know."

"There, there", said Mrs. Meyer putting her arms round her as she had never done before. "Things aren't always the way they sometimes seem."

"Why did you collect all those seeds if you don't want to plant them?"

"I would like to, but my back won't allow it."

"I can help you!" Eli suddenly felt the urge to create a new flower bed. "Will you show me how to do it correctly?"

The old lady looked so happy, as if she had waited her whole life for this very request. "I'd love to, when the time is right."

From day to day the garden was growing happier and more colourful, without anyone's help. On the inside window sill, marigolds were starting to germinate in yoghurt and cream pots and little tomato plants grew in discarded cottage cheese cartons.

Eli could hardly wait to start laying out her flower bed. Even Nick seemed to have been bitten by something: within an hour he had talked more than he normally did in a whole week. But maybe it was because Eli listened to him more carefully as she sat quietly beside him and looked, and marvelled that there were so many new things to be discovered. The crocuses had delicate purple stripes and flowers as yellow as the sun and daffodils trumpeted their scent all over the meadow where snowdrops were making room for cowslips. The cowslip's fragrance mixed with that of wild violets and pansies sat on their beds like little clowns. Nemesia nodded by the wall, and campions and fluffy cotton grass greeted the mild air from across the pond, and then on this, the most beautiful day of all, the old cherry tree blossomed. It appeared to be wearing a white silk dress. Honey bees and bumble bees hummed so loudly they could be heard as far as pond and Eli and Nick could gaze though the flowers all the way up into the blue sky. How lovely it was going to be to harvest those delicious cherries in the summer!

But wait: had Grandma Mary not said two trees were needed for that?

"Yes, that's right: sweet cherries are not self-pollenating", Mrs. Meyer explained when Eli approached her somewhat distraught. "But don't worry, two streets away from here is another splendid specimen. That should be enough to secure a reasonable harvest."

Eli clapped her hands in excitement. "So when are we finally going to plant the marigolds outside?"

"When the time is right."

"And when's that?"

"When the sun's strong enough."

"And when is that?"

"Winter could still return, you know."

"The flower lady has put all her flowers into the yard."

"She surely puts them back inside at night."

"I could do that, too!"

Eli fetched two pots with marigolds and put them on the terrace table. "You will see: they are sure to grow much faster here than inside! And they look really pretty, too."

Mrs. Meyer smiled. "I hope you don't forget them."

"Certainly not!"

Eli jumped down the steps whooping with joy and ran across to the flowering garden.

"Yippiee, hooray! Spring has finally arrived!"

The following days proved the opposite. Snow flurries fell, rain seemed to wash all the colours away, the sky was grey and the wind was as icy as if it was November. Actually, it was worse than November because from November one could not expect anything different. When Eli returned to the garden the unfortunate marigolds had frozen to death.

"You put them outside although you didn't have the time to look after them", Mrs. Meyer said. This was less an accusation, more of a friendly statement of fact.

Sadly Eli carried the black remains over to the compost.

"We should be looking after the olive tree", Mrs. Meyer said when she returned.

"Olives only grow in the South!" Eli knew that because Pa had explained to her where the oil came from that Ma put on her salads.

"Sometimes they grow here, too", Mrs. Meyer said. She went to one of the sheds behind the house which was hidden so well that Eli had not discovered it before. Under the eaves was a huge present. It was more than double Eli's size, wrapped in a beige tarpaulin and tied with a bow of sackcloth. Mrs. Meyer undid the bow and pulled off the tarpaulin. Out came a big pot with a little tree. The narrow trunk was embedded in straw; the bark was covered with small cracks and on the branches hung sad black and brown leaves. There was no question: the poor olive tree had suffered the same fate as the marigolds.

"Maybe you didn't wrap it up warmly enough?"

Mrs. Meyer removed the straw. "We had a bitter winter." She said as she folded the tarpaulin and Eli helped to take the straw to the compost. "Would you like some mint tea?" Mrs. Meyer asked on the way back. Eli nodded, but her thoughts were with the little olive tree. The old lady disappeared into the house and Eli sat down on the terrace. After all, it was comforting to know that even a very wise Mrs. Meyer made mistakes. And the olive tree was surely more precious than two yoghurt pots of marigolds.

"What are you going to do with it?" Eli asked when she had finished her tea.

"Wait."

Mrs. Meyer stacked the dishes and took them inside. Eli walked back to the shed. The little tree really looked sad. You could peel the bark off the narrow trunk and the leaves were just as sad shadows on the shed wall. If this sight was too much for Eli, how did Mrs. Meyer feel about it? Best to rid the world of evil! Maybe if one did not have to look at it, it would not be as bad any more. Eli had already experienced that feeling with the marigolds.

She went and fetched the hedge clippers, cut off all branches and hid them under the bushes by the wall. She had to look for the saw to

cut up the trunk and was sweating when she had finished. Suddenly Mrs. Meyer was standing beside her.

"Why did you do that?"

"Because it's dead."

"How do you know that?"

"Because a tree cannot live without its bark. And this one's peeling off almost by itself! And all the leaves were brown but Pa said that olives always have green leaves and they can't tolerate severe frost. And a severe frost we had."

The old lady took Eli's hand placed it upon the sawn-off stump. It felt damp. She scratched the remaining bark and underneath it there was a green shimmer.

"You see: there's still sap."

Eli looked at her horrified. "Does that mean something would have become of it? That it would have grown new leaves if I hadn't … was it still alive?"

"One can never tell. There's much that would speak against it, and some for it. To discover the right answer you should have had a little more patience."

Eli felt the tears welling in her eyes. "But why didn't you tell me before?"

"You didn't ask."

That had been a sad day, but then came a day that was even worse. Even worse than the day when robber chieftain Matt shouted that he no longer had a daughter. He believed that Ronia had betrayed him, but it had not been true. But it was true for Eli, just the other way round.

Actually, it was a beautiful day with fluffy cotton-wool clouds sailing across bright ocean-blue sky. Eli looked up and began to dream. She had attended therapy, but by now had run out of answers to the countless questions of the red-bespectacled doctor and, anyway, she did not feel like repeating everything twice or even three times over. That was why she had finished early that day.

When she unlocked the door to Pa's flat, she could hear him talking loudly in the kitchen. A woman answered just as loudly. Eli

recognized the voice immediately. What was Kate doing here? And why were they fighting?

The kitchen door was ajar and Eli crept closer. She could see a part of Pa's back and nothing of Kate.

"You have to tell her!" Kate shouted.

"But I just can't", said Pa.

"I'm not going to be part of this mess any longer!"

"Kate, please. Eli isn't ready yet."

"And when is she going to be ready for it? In three years, in five? Ten? When she's had her third child at thirty?"

Eli could feel a raging temper rising up inside her. What was this silly cow thinking?

"If you don't tell her, I will!" she shouted, sounding really angry.

"You won't!" said Pa, sounding just as annoyed.

"Can't you see that your lying to her is making it worse? You pretend there's a world that doesn't exist!" Kate laughed scornfully. "You pretended to you looked for lucky clover for her. If I had known the sort of a fairy-tale you were making up, I would have thrown the dusty things out."

Pop's voice softened. "Look: for you, those clover leaves don't mean anything anymore, for my little girl they are something really special."

"Oh, for heaven's sake! Just because she believes, her saintly Pa picked them himself in the moonlight! What is she going to say when she hears that my ex once gave me those for our wedding?" Now her voice became softer, too. "For our own sake: tell your daughter the truth. She is old enough to understand."

Eli was paralyzed with horror. Pa had lied to her from the outset! And he obviously wanted to replace Ma with Kate! She felt tears running down her cheeks. And then a big lump grew in her throat making her feel as though she could not breathe. Pa and Kate kept on talking, but Eli did not want to hear any more. She just wanted to get away and never see Pa again. Actually, she did not want to see anyone in the whole world, ever again.

She hung the coloured string with the key onto the coat rack, closed the door of the flat behind her and ran down the stairs into

the street. The sky was not blue anymore and the clouds were hanging grey and heavy above the houses.

Pop betrayed me, pounded inside her head whilst she ran in the direction that she believed was the right one. Ma was working, she would not miss Eli. She would probably not even miss her if she did not come back at all! Neither would Pa. He now had Kate. A voice inside her told her that this was not true, but it was surely lying, just like Pa had! And it was just as much Ma's fault as well, that everything was the way it was now. No, she would definitely not go home! At this moment there was only one place she wanted to be.

Eli stopped and looked around. She had never been in this street before. Sullenly, she wiped her tears away. Ronia would be able to find the way forward!

The clouds were still grey and black and her feet ached unbearably when she finally reached the piece of grass in front of the wall. She slipped through the gap in the wall and felt almost immediately better. It was as if the old garden with its leaves and flowers, sounds and smells was weaving a soft cloak of comfort and security around her.

Eli listened to the gurgling of the little stream and watched the hurried water skaters. She did not call for Luigi. Today was not a day to travel to the sky. Finally, she went over to the cherry tree and sat down in the grass beside Nick. Not only had Pa betrayed her: now she knew that he and Ma would never get back together again, no matter how much she wished for it.

She cried and Nick listened to her tears.

"I am so unhappy", she sobbed when finally no more tears were left.

He blinked. "Looking at the sky, I think I am, too. We are going to have one hell of a thunderstorm."

"I don't care about the thunderstorm!" Eli cried. "My Pa lied to me and he betrayed me!"

"Those clouds look dreadful."

"He gave me a lucky clover and pretended he had picked it especially for me. But it's not true!"

Nick straightened his pointed cap. "Lucky clover is called lucky clover because it has four leaves instead of three, right? And if I understand correctly: yours still has them."

Eli was getting annoyed. "You're making fun of me!"

"What makes you think I'm making fun of you?"

"You look as though you are."

"Is it alright for you if I say I'm not?"

"But you look as if you are", Eli insisted.

"Maybe it would be convenient for you if I looked as though I was? So you can be really angry with me?"

Eli started to wonder whether Nick was the right one to be talking to about all her troubles. And so she just sat beside him leaning on the trunk of the old cherry tree and said nothing more. But maybe saying nothing was exactly what she needed most at this moment.

CHAPTER NINE

The sky looked scary. There were ink-black clouds and it rumbled and crashed as if God was re-arranging the furniture. Blasts of wind swirled the leaves through the air, twisted and bent twigs and branches, and tousled Eli's hair. She got up and ran towards the house. Mrs. Meyer was not there and Eli did not want to go in without her. She curled up in the rocking chair. Heavy drops splashed onto the balustrade and more gusts swept through the whole garden. Eli wrapped her arms around her legs and was glad the terrace was covered. Suddenly, it started to pour down as if heaven was emptying bathtubs full of water, it pelted down on the roof so hard that Eli had to cover her ears. It sounded like a bunch of naughty boys throwing pebbles, but it was hailstones followed by blinding flashes of lightning and massive thunder claps, so much so, that Eli was at a loss at what to be afraid of most. It seemed to her that it took forever before the awe-inspiring thunderstorm finally moved on.

Then the sun managed to prise the clouds apart with an almost poisonous yellow, as if someone up there had turned on a dim ugly light, and Eli could not believe what she saw: the old garden was white – and leafless! Thousands of delicate spring leaves lay smashed beneath the trees and bushes and the few that still remained were riddled with appallingly ragged holes. But the flowers looked even worse: blooms had been cruelly slaughtered, stalks bent and broken. It really had been an inferno of a storm – Nick had been right. And he was actually worse off than she.

He was not able to run away and nor could the trees and flowers either. They had to endure whatever came along, even if it was death by hailstones. Eli wanted to cry again. First Pa had left her and now

the garden was utterly devastated, too. This world was not fair! Nick sat surrounded by a pile of hail and shredded leaves.

"Isn't this awful?" Eli shouted.

He opened one eye. "Isn't this wonderful?" Eli was about to ask him if he was in his right mind but then she saw it too: a huge rainbow stretched across the whole garden. It was amazing that a wicked thunderstorm could create something so beautiful! She turned towards Nick, but he had already pulled his cap over his face and fallen asleep. This troll was completely and utterly impossible!

Down at the pond she called for Luigi and sighed with relief when she heard his funny toot. Ice was stuck to one of the tree stumps, but Luigi did not seem to mind. He exhaled a little cloud of steam.

"Do you want to travel with me to the sky?" How could he think of pleasure amidst this terrible destruction and be in such an awfully good mood?

"No, I do not!" said Eli, but the little train did not leave her alone until she finally climbed aboard. She pulled the curtains too in an effort to shut out the chaos. It was no use. Luigi cut the corners at such a speed that the windows burst open and the head wind blew the curtains aside. As previously, everything that had been small before got bigger. And not just the size changed: the rough hailstones changed into glittering magic balls and as they travelled over the bent blades of grass, the raindrops slid off like pearls from a green string.

Across Nick's pointed cap they went, into the wet ivy by the cherry tree trunk and all the way up from branch to branch until they flew through a hole in a jagged cherry tree leaf straight towards the rainbow. Up close, the colours looked even brighter and did not just cover the garden, but arced over the whole town. The multi-coloured arch radiated as if wanting to outshine all the troubles of the world.

On her way home, Eli was still sad, but at the same time a bit happy. If it had not been so boring at the doctors, she would not have left early and then she still would not know that Pa lied and betrayed her. And if Pa had not lied and betrayed her, she would not have been in the garden. And if it had not been for the hailstorm, she would not have travelled with Luigi through the battered cherry tree leaf to the rainbow. Ma and Pa sat at the kitchen table. If this had happened

yesterday, Eli would have been happy, but now she knew that that it meant nothing and it never would. Ma jumped up. "Where have you been all this time?"

Pop did not say anything. He just looked tired and sad.

"Went for a walk", Eli said.

"In this weather?"

"I was at Emma's", Eli lied.

Pop looked at her. "You heard me talking to Kate, didn't you?"

Eli felt that lump swelling again, but this time it was not quite as large. She shrugged and went to her room. Pa followed her.

"Please believe me: I have wanted to tell you for a long time but as you didn't seem to like Kate, I didn't dare."

"You lied to me!"

"Yes", he admitted. "Can you ever forgive me?"

Eli took the parchment bag with the clover from Ronia's book. "You can give this dusty rubbish back to your Kate."

She saw that her words made him even sadder, but he could not possibly be as sad as she already was!

He put the little bag into his pocket. "It would be nice if you could understand one day ..."

"I understand that you prefer living with this stupid Kate to living with Ma!"

Eli stared out of the window. The wilted snowdrops in the yoghurt pots looked just as miserable as she felt. She jumped as she felt his hands on her shoulders. She had always felt protected and safe when he did that; now it was a heavy burden, one that she would have liked to shake off.

"Whatever happens, you will always be my brave little Ronia", he said softly, but Eli knew that that was exactly what she no longer was.

The whole day had been like a hailstorm and it had destroyed much more than just the flowers in Mrs. Meyer's garden. And Nick and Luigi had comforted her - not Pa.

He removed his hands. "Would you prefer to be by yourself?"

Eli nodded. Since Christmas, this was the second time she was glad when he left. She pushed Mimi aside and opened the window. The rainbow had disappeared, and with it the last little speck of hap-

piness: she did not have anywhere to hide anymore! She threw herself on the bed, crying, and sobbed herself to sleep. She dreamed of Ronia and of Matt's Wood and there was terrific thunder and lightning and then she slid down the rainbow with Pa and Nick and they splashed from the cherry tree straight into the pond. And Grandma Mary sat in Mrs. Meyer's rocking chair, the birds sang and Luigi hovered above in the woolly clouds.

During the following weeks, Eli spent a lot of time with Emma. She felt it was a lot better to think about maths problems and essays than about Pa's lies, and Mrs. Meyer's destroyed garden. Anyway, Eli needed to work a bit more for school because her last dictation had been a disaster.

When she confided with Emma she did not want to go to therapy any more, she answered: "Then don't go." It was almost funny to hear so much rebelliousness from the mouth of such a well-behaved, model pupil. But she was right! Neither Ma nor Pa could bring Eli to attend another session with the red-bespectacled doctor. Pa wanted to return her key, but Eli said she did not need it because she was not going to visit him again. She knew she hurt him by saying that, but that was exactly what she wanted. The former robber chieftain should experience what it felt like to be abandoned! Unfortunately, this did not help much because Eli was still sad and missed him more and more every day. But she would never have admitted it!

It was surprising that Emma, of all people, should be the one who was best able to take her mind off her troubles: she showed Eli her favourite books, but there were no stories about secret gardens, robbers and princes, only numbers and digits, though she did teach Eli some useful tricks on how to remember much of it. She talked and explained until Eli's head was spinning and there was not another millimetre of space left for sad thoughts. The days passed and when Eli returned home from school on the Friday she had almost forgotten about Pa and the old garden. In the flat it was chilly; Ma said they had to save on heating cost. Eli ate a yoghurt and went into her room. She had deliberately left the curtains closed so she did not have to constantly see the cherry tree. She now pulled them back and stared

at Mimi: with all Emma's stories, garden sadness and Pa madness, she had not remembered to water her and now the poor leaves hung limply down as those of the lucky clover had done in winter. But maybe she could be saved? In the hope that Mimi would revive, Eli poured water into the little sunny yellow pot until the under tray overflowed – but as it turned out, without success.

"Some things cannot be mended", the flower lady said when Eli took the sad remains over to her on Saturday morning.

"But what am I going to do now?" she cried desperately.

"Maybe think about whether a mimosa really is the right plant for you?"

Eli wiped an errant tear from her eye. "But I really loved her."

The flower lady emptied Mimi and her soil into a bucket. "Loving isn't enough. She needs to be looked after and cared for too."

The lump in Eli's throat was too large to talk.

On Monday, she decided to go back to the garden. After therapy had ceased, only the tennis coach excuse remained. Emma looked disappointed, but Eli's guilty conscience was soon forgotten as she slipped through the gap in the wall. She was afraid of what awaited her. Afraid that the garden, like Mimi, was not to be mended anymore; that she had lost it, as she had lost Pa – but what was that?

Behind the wall everything blossomed and flourished as if the hailstorm had never been! Only on closer inspection could she see the scars of the past destruction: severed green cherries lay moulding in the grass, a frayed leaf between delicate fresh ones, bent stalks, a flower without petals. Much fresh new life had begun to push its way through, she could not believe her eyes. Near the terrace there were bright red tulips and a sea of forget-me-nots, the meadow was a sunny yellow sea of dandelions and the path to the pavilion was covered with daisies. It was as if the garden was painting a new Today over the grey old Yesterday.

Eli visited Mrs. Meyer almost every day and each time the garden became greener and greener. The shrubs by the wall grew rampant, forming a thorny tunnel though which it became difficult for Eli to squeeze. The light green Christmas roses were soon overgrown by rich green ground elder, ivy and hops clambered up the bushes and

trees forming green rooms, which, depending on whether the sun was shining or clouds passing, had blue or white ceilings. And from those rooms soft songs could be heard of the wind, peculiar ones of birds and the loud frogs whose croaking was audible even beyond the wall in Ma's flat.

As the mint thrived in abundance, it gave Mrs. Meyer a daily crop and when Eli went to see Nick after tea, the grass smelled of hay and honey.

One sunny day in May, Mrs. Meyer finally moved the cottage cheese cartons and yoghurt pots outside.

"Is the time right now?" Eli asked

The old lady smiled and nodded and they spent the whole afternoon planting marigolds and tomatoes in the terrace bed replacing the now withered tulips and forget-me-nots. Eli was disappointed with the seemingly meagre results, but said nothing.

In the meadow, sunny heads of the dandelions changed into fluffy dandelion clocks and grass outgrew the daisies. More and more mysterious corners and hiding places were appearing in the old garden, overgrown paths, intertwined thickets and thorny canopies where robin redbreasts, wrens and hedgehogs lived. But the brightly coloured flowers, which Eli had so loved in Grandma Mary's garden, were lacking. Instead, ground elder and couch grass sprouted everywhere and clumps of stinging nettles proliferated.

"Grandma Mary always said you have to watch out that weeds don't grow up over your head", said Eli, whilst eating the first nettle soup of the year.

Mrs. Meyer nodded. "Yes. It's about time to start preparing your new flower bed." Eli helped herself to another ladle of soup. Like Grandma Mary, Mrs. Meyer had used cream, a blob of yoghurt and a good pinch of nutmeg; they had fresh bread with it and it tasted delicious.

"I am going to have the most beautiful flowers far and wide!" exclaimed Eli still chewing. "And lots of strawberries and raspberries! Maybe even red currants, but definitely not the black ones: Grandma Mary always made them into juice, which she gave to me whenever

I had a cold. That's why I always had to make sure I didn't sneeze when I visited."

Mrs. Meyer laughed. "You need to decide whether you prefer a flower bed or a berries patch. Where would you like us to actually put it?"

"By the wall, right beside the mint!"

"Why there?"

"Because then I can enjoy looking and smelling at the same time."

Mrs. Meyer wanted to say something, but then changed her mind. Eli emptied her plate and helped clean the dishes. After that, they carried hoe, spade, rake and a bucket from the pavilion over to the wall.

"Before you start, you need to consider what you would like to have where", said Mrs. Meyer.

Eli took the hoe. "Why? First the weeds have to go and then I'll plant the flowers. That's how Grandma Mary always used to do it."

"Which flowers is it to be?"

Eli could remember the colours in Grandma Mary's garden, but not their proper names.

"Red, yellow and blue ones of course – and then a few that flower orange and purple. And I need some greens, too. It's going to be a big rainbow bed you know!"

"Hm", said Mrs. Meyer. "If you have questions or need help: I'm on the terrace." She left and Eli was happy to able to finally get started.

Gleefully, she started hacking away at the weeds. Dearie me, they were stubborn! Well, if the roots didn't want to leave the ground, she would just pull the leaves off. Ground elder could be eaten at a pinch - at least Grandma Mary had said so, and with regard to those nettles: the soup had been so delicious that it was quite useful to have fresh ones grow back again anyway. Besides, with it she already had the green needed for her rainbow bed. Eli hacked and dug, and dug and hacked, so much so that her back and hands started to really ache.

By the evening, despite all her determination and toil, still only a narrow strip of weeds was cleared so Eli decided that a small rainbow bed would be a lot nicer anyway.

The following day she went to the flower lady after school. "Would you happen to have a few flower bed plants leftover for me?"

"What sort are you looking for?"

"Well, pretty, colourful ones."

The flower lady grinned. "If your colourful and pretty flowers are supposed to match, you will have to tell me a little more."

"Match what?" asked Eli in wonder.

"As you probably know, there are not only plants with small or large, simple or double blossoms; some of them need lots of sun, others grow in the shade and then again some don't mind either. And they flower at different times of the year."

Eli had never thought about this. She suddenly felt quite stupid. "It's only a small bed", she said sheepishly. "Close to a wall."

"A wall – so that means it's rather shady?"

"It does get a little sun."

"So, half-shade. Is the earth dry or moist?"

"Aaah ... moist, I believe, or, at least it was yesterday when I was hacking away the weeds."

"What sort of weeds were they?"

"Ground elder and stinging nettles, why?"

"Some weeds prefer certain types of soil that others don't", the flower lady explained. "That's how they tell us which other plants might flourish in the same place."

Eli had found it exhausting enough digging up the weeds and now she was supposed to think about the type of soil it preferred? She had never thought making a rainbow bed would be so complicated. Maybe it would be more rewarding to plant berries?

"Do you have raspberries and strawberries? And maybe currants – but only the red ones?"

"Raspberries are planted in the autumn", the flower lady explained. "And strawberries preferably in late summer. To make them taste well they need lots of sun - currants do too, by the way. But ferns would grow nicely in front of a wall."

"Ferns are boring", Eli said. Besides, there were enough in the garden already.

"Boring? Well, then come with me." The flower lady led Eli into a little garden behind the shop where lots of pots stood around full of ugly looking ochre coloured lumps. Eli pulled a face; the flower lady smiled. "Wait and see!" She pointed to the different pots and gave them such funny names, Eli had to laugh: "Asparagus fern, Bear's Paw Fern, Stripy Fern, Birds Nest Fern, Squirrel-foot Fern, Brake Fern, Maidenhair Fern, Hawaiian Tree Fern, Holly Fern, Staghorn Fern." And then as she told a story about each one, the lumps started to unfurl before Eli's very eyes and turned into a green enchanted forest.

"I can't have colourful flowers in my bed", she said when she got back to Mrs. Meyer's garden.

The old lady peeked inquisitively into the little box Eli had placed on the terrace table. "So what other pretty things did you bring instead?"

"Funny ferns. Will you help me plant them?"

They planted the lumps quickly and the result looked even more pathetic than the tomatoes growing in front of the terrace. The magic of all those beautiful names had vanished; Eli felt disappointment and a little angry. "It's such a pity I cannot have my rainbow bed."

"My dear child! Why does it have to be in that shady place near the wall?"

"Everywhere else is overgrown!"

Mrs. Meyer put the hoe back into the empty box. "Wasn't it overgrown here before, too? Why not look for a sunny place where things will grow which you feel are worth less than your colourful flowers."

"But then I will have to start digging again!"

The old lady smiled. "There may be wishes that fulfil themselves, for yours you'll need to sweat a little more. But don't worry, you will have forgotten it by the time your rainbow blossoms start to flower."

"Yes", Eli said apathetically. Her back still hurt from yesterday's efforts and her hands were full of blisters.

"How would you like to have a bed by the terrace?" Mrs. Meyer suggested. "The first colours are already there with your marigolds; you could add some larkspur, asters, phlox and daylilies - daylilies taste delicious, by the way!" She winked. "Sometimes you can help the fulfilling of wishes along a little. Besides, there are wishes that come true without you realising it - or before they are even wished for." As they walked to the shed behind the house, Eli was looking

bewildered. There was string stretched along the shed wall, not far from the pot with the remains of dead olive tree. Below them, some stalks had started to sprout. "Raspberries", Mrs. Meyer said. "And red, white and black currants are growing in the front garden near the pergola. There are strawberries, too, but only the miniature wild ones. And those thorny vines over there are blackberries. You'll have to try them in July. They are delicious." Her wrinkles twinkled. "But before we start tackling the terrace, we should harvest couple of cups of tea, don't you think?"

Summer.

If you think of angels, they will
move their wings.

from Israel

CHAPTER TEN

The ferns with the funny names quickly took over the bed by the wall and Eli was content. The flower lady had been right: they were pretty enough, but Eli's rainbow bed by the terrace was just unsurpassably beautiful! The marigolds were all shades of colour from red to orange to bright yellow, the larkspurs the flower lady had selected would soon be flowering light blue, dark blue and purple in amongst green growing rapidly into a great archway over Mrs. Meyer's home-grown tomatoes. It didn't matter that they weren't actually flowers because, if what the old lady had claimed were true, there would be red, yellow, striped and purple ones shaped like globes, bottles or cones and would taste delicious.

So far, they had only strewn a little pale yellow and green of their leaves into Eli's colourful dance, but here and there one could already make out small fruit. And where else would you be able to find an edible rainbow?

These days, whenever Eli came to the garden, she always visited the terrace first, except this one afternoon in early June. She stood speechless: the brush with its thorny vines, its green tangle that overgrew trees and shrubs gradually burying the pavilion, the wall and the pergola beneath; the one that she had often ranted about because it suffocated the flowers, the one that tore her skin and clothes if she didn't watch out – had overnight turned into a sea of flowers. A sea of many thousands of petals from delicate rosé to rich pinks, bright red and gleaming whites, cream and sunrise-yellows. It was as if a painter had mixed together the colours of the sun and moon, and fire and snow on his palette; again and again in ever new shades, then daubed it so lavishly onto a rich green base that even Eli's rainbow bed seemed only a speck within this riotous multitude. A sweet aro-

ma mingled with a hint of freshly squeezed lemon covered everything almost like a varnish. Even Nick beamed: the roses were flowering – summer was here!

Since Eli did not just come to the old garden to gaze, but to work too, she often had the feeling that this vivid green world was just waiting for her to take it on, that it all belonged to her and she could shape and form it at will. It was a wonderful feeling and if Ma had not moved to that boring street with her, if Pa had not left, she would never have experienced it.

And so it was that Mrs. Meyer's garden somehow also helped her make peace with Pa. No, it was not that she could forgive him for his betrayal yet, and she would never get used to Kate, but she did not mind him picking her up from school in the afternoon, once a week. This is when they went to the zoo together, had ice cream or chips at the Little Jug, but this was only if it was Kate's day off.

Eli was pleasant to Pa and Pa was pleasant enough to her, but it seemed as if a hedge hat grown between them, and with every new leaf that grew, the more the memories of those beautiful times they had had when living together disappeared from view.

Eli had previously drawn on every one of the few hours she could spend with him, but now she did not mind if he sometimes could not make it. Then she just went to the garden. Or to see Emma.

Despite Emma being a strange girl and the other children not liking her, it was not a reason for not doing homework with her, combining practicality with pleasure: her mummy made a delicious lunch and from Emma's balcony, although you could not actually look into the old garden itself, you could see the cherries in the higher branches of the tree turning red.

Eli did not need tennis lessons anymore as Emma now knew she was going to the forbidden garden. Eli had tried to persuade her to come along, but Emma did not dare. Instead, she helped Eli now and again with a little white lie if Ma was looking for her. Eli appreciated this because, although Eli herself did not have a guilty conscience if it was anything to do with the garden, she knew that even harmless little fibs meant quite an effort for good-as-gold Emma. Maybe that was what connected the two of them: that there

was no connection between them. And so they sat on the balcony after school and each of them told the other what she thought and felt, what she wished for, what she liked and disliked and because the one did not really understand the other, at some point they started to quarrel.

"Really, those numbers are a strange habit of yours."

"Really, that garden thing is a strange habit of yours."

"You're nuts!"

"If anyone here is nuts, it's you."

"Definitely not!"

"Definitely yes."

"No!"

"Yes!"

June sparkled with lots of sun, just as the May had done, and one sunny-sky-blue day the cherries were finally ripe! But only those way up high in the crown of the tree. Seductively, they glared down at Eli in the garden.

"Wait a little longer", Nick advised. "Two or three more days and the ones down here will be ripe, too, and an easy pick."

Eli shook her head. She had waited long enough! On her third attempt, she managed to climb all the way up the trunk to the top and shortly afterwards sat proudly and happily on a forked branch, surrounded by red, plump fruit. She pulled off a twinned red couple, separated them and with great relish popped her first self-picked cherry into her mouth. How sweet and juicy it was! No wonder Pa had loved cherries. She sucked the flesh from the stone and spat it through the branches high into the sky. The second one tasted even better, the third was more delicious again and the fourth incomparable!

Eli picked, ate and spat, ate, picked and spat and stopped only when her tummy began to rebel. She picked another handful for the road, climbed back down again and slumped satisfied into the grass beside Nick. She offered him a cherry. "Here. Why don't you try."

"No thanks", he resisted. "I'll wait until they come voluntarily."

"But when they fall off by themselves, they are usually all mushy! And it takes forever."

Nick looked at the fern. "I like it if it takes a while. That way I can enjoy the wait for the delight."

Eli shook her head and went over to the terrace.

Mrs. Meyer was pleased to do without the waiting. Smiling, she took a cherry from Eli's hand and Eli forgot about her tummy and ate yet another one. The old lady munched and rolled the stone from one side of her cheek to the other with an expression on her face that must have been similar to Ronia's when she decided that she had to practice not being afraid.

"I bet I can get further than you!" She said, spitting the cherry stone over the larkspur and marigolds all the way into the pond.

Eli laughed so much that the rest of the cherries rolled from her hands. Together, they picked them up again and Eli spat her stone over the balustrade. It landed between the tomatoes.

Mrs. Meyer managed to catapult the second stone even further. Eli did the same, into the tomatoes again. Mrs. Meyer's wrinkles looked mischievous. "You know we are doing something very noble here?"

"Nope." Upon her third attempt, Eli barely missed the border of the flower bed.

Mrs. Meyer was definitely leading. "In old times, cherries were very precious", she said. "Only rich nobles could afford this expensive fruit. And if uninvited guests sneaked in amongst the crowd, as sometimes happened, those elegant ladies and gentlemen started spitting stones and stems at them until they fled. That's why we still have the saying today: not everyone likes to share their cherries."

Eli smiled. "You'll have to tell Emma that story. I'm going to bring her along tomorrow."

Mrs. Meyer looked at her sternly. "Oh, I wouldn't do that."

"But why not? These cherries are so delicious! Once Emma has tried them, she is going to like the garden just as much as I do."

"Why do you so desperately want her to like the garden?"

Eli thought for a moment. "Because it's so wonderful to be here. And as I'm sure every person likes to eat cherries!"

"Oh yes? How many of these persons do you know?"

"You should be happy Emma's coming along", Eli said huffily. "Because then you can tell her she's wrong."

"What is it you think she's wrong about?"

"She keeps arguing that you died a long time ago!"

"So what would change if she came here?" It was such a silly question that Eli preferred not to answer.

"Look out over the garden", Eli said, whilst sitting with Emma on the balcony after lunch the following day.

Absent-mindedly, Emma looked up from her maths book. "Why?"

"The cherries are ripe."

"Mhmm." Emma murmured and continued, immersed in her facts and figures.

"They taste delicious!"

"It is forbidden to go into the garden."

"It's wonderful to go into the garden! What do you say we go and say hello to Nick and for dessert we'll pick some of those scrumptious cherries."

"I don't climb trees."

"Then we'll take a ride up to the top."

"You're mad."

"And after that we'll have a cup of strawberry and mint tea with Mrs. Meyer."

"Mrs. Meyer is dead."

"No, she isn't!"

"Yes, she is!"

"No, she isn't. Come with me and I'll prove it to you."

"And who's Nick?"

"Come on, come with me and I'll show you."

Emma put her book aside and screwed the top back on her fountain pen. "Well alright then, let's go this minute."

Eli jumped up and hugged her. "You'll love it!"

Shortly afterwards, the two crept across the piece of barren land, where by now the grass had grown as high as it had in the garden. Eli, being careful to make sure no one watched, let Emma go in first.

"Ouch!"

"What is it?" Eli asked

"I scratched myself! There are thorns everywhere!"

"Good heavens! Can you please not make so much noise?"

They climbed in one after the other. Inside, Eli proudly spread out her arms and declared. "Isn't it wonderful?"

Emma looked down. "Oh dear! My pretty socks are quite torn."

"Stop making such a fuss!" Eli said becoming mildly annoyed and went down to the pond.

Grumbling, Emma followed. "They cost a lot of money, you know."

Eli crouched down by the tree stump.

"Luigi - are you there?" Eli called. "Luigi, proud ship: come on out!"

"What are you doing?" Emma asked.

"I would like to introduce you to my friend Luigi. He believes he is a ship, but actually he is a tiny train, he lives underneath those roots."

"Are you trying to have me on?"

"No!"

But no matter how often Eli called, Luigi was nowhere to be seen. Maybe it was because today you could not hear the gurgling of the little stream? Eli stood up. "Can you believe that I travelled through a cherry tree leaf with him, all the way up to a rainbow?"

"Hm", was all Emma said. She sounded almost like the red-bespectacled doctor.

"All right then. Let's visit Nick", Eli decided.

They went towards the cherry tree.

"Ouch!" said Emma.

"What is it now?"

"There are stinging nettles everywhere! Really, Eli: this is not a garden, this is wilderness! And I can't see what you like so much about it. Come on, let's go back. We have homework to finish."

"We have enough time to do our stupid homework later!" Eli replied and stomped on ahead, but by the time they reached the cherry tree, her anger was forgotten. Nick leaned against the trunk; his eyes

were closed, the legs crossed, hands folded in his lap and his cap sat lopsided on his head. Eli stood in front of him smiling.

"Nick, wake up! I would like to introduce you to Emma."

Emma looked at Eli flabbergasted. "You're not trying to tell me you talk to that ugly stone gnome?"

"Nick is a troll!" Eli said indignantly. "And he moved here from Sweden especially, and he has clever answers to a lot of complicated questions." That was not entirely true of course, but Eli had to say at least something in defence of her friend. On the other hand: why did he not defend himself? Why was he sitting there, as if carved of stone and didn't say a word?

Emma folded her arms in front of her chest. "Well really: this is getting idiotic."

Eli pointed to the cherry tree. "I am going to pick some. Are you coming?"

"I've told you before: I don't climb trees! Anyway, I'd never be able make it all the way up there." She was right for a change, clumsy as she was.

"I will pick some for you too", Eli said being mildly patronising.

This time she only needed one attempt and was able to climb a lot faster than the previous day.

"Careful! You're going to fall!" Emma called out anxiously.

"No way", Eli replied, throwing a few cherries down onto the grass. Emma picked one up and prising it open examined it suspiciously.

"What are you doing?" Eli asked astonished.

"I'm looking if ... yuk!" Emma dropped the cherry in disgust. It landed right on Nick's head, but not even that seemed to disturb him. "Yukyyuk", she screamed. "There're lots of disgusting maggots in there!"

Eli climbed back down.

"Please be quiet! The whole street is going to be after us if they hear you scream like that! Anyway, what you're saying is nonsense. I have eaten at least one bucket full and there was nothing nasty there."

"Have a look yourself!"

Eli took another cherry from her trouser pocket and opened it with her fingers.

"So? Am I right?" Emma asked.

"Nope." Eli said, bravely popping the cherry into her mouth and swallowing it, stone and all. "And now we're going to see Mrs. Meyer."

They followed the path up to the house and climbed the rotting stairs onto the terrace. The French windows were closed and the rocking chair abandoned.

"And Mrs. Meyer is supposed to live here?" Emma asked in disbelief.

Eli shook her head. "She's only visiting." She rattled the door. "Well, okay. Let's try round the back."

"Eli, please! Can't you see this house is unoccupied? Everything inside is bound to be full of dust and dirt!"

"I sat here only yesterday with Mrs. Meyer and we ate cherries. And we drank mint tea!"

"Yes, yes. And you also travelled to the sky on a train that really is a ship, and talk to an old stone statue." Eli could not stop the tears welling up in her eyes. She ran off leaving Emma standing. Why had she taken the silly cow along in the first place? How on earth could she have imagined that Emma would understand what she experienced and felt in the garden?

Emma caught up with her just beyond the wall. "Don't be angry with me. It's just that all you said sounded very strange." Eli almost flew off the handle again, but Emma held her hands. "I really don't care if you talk to stones or take rides to the rainbow, just as long as we're friends."

She sounded so very innocent and sincere that Eli's anger evaporated. What had happened in the old garden was quite incredible, and she really should not have been angry with Emma, but with Nick, Luigi and Mrs. Meyer instead.

"Let's go back to the balcony", Emma said. "I'll show you how that maths problem can be solved and my mummy will make us some delicious mint tea." Eli nodded. There was no point in trying to tell Emma that the freshly picked leaves from Mrs. Meyer's garden tasted

a hundred times better than the flavourless stuff you could buy in the shops.

The following day after school, Eli's path led her directly to the garden. Nick lounged amongst the ferns looking at the sky.

Eli placed herself demonstrably in front of him. "Why didn't you talk to me yesterday?"

"Should I have done?" he asked.

"I wanted to introduce you to my friend Emma. And what did you do? You sat there like a stone sculpture!"

"I am a stone sculpture."

"But you're talking to me! Why didn't you talk to her?"

"Why is it so important to you that I talk to her?"

"Because she thinks I'm just imagining everything."

"What's so bad about her believing that?"

"You all let me down! Luigi wasn't there, Mrs. Meyer wasn't around either and you didn't say a word!"

"But I'm talking to you now."

Eli gave up. She went to the pond and called out for Luigi.

"Trillala, Trullala", came the sound from the depths of the root and soon the little train appeared chugging across the moss, huffing and puffing.

"Hello, Eli! Jump in and we'll take a ride to the sky."

"So, today you're here!" Eli said enraged. "And where were you yesterday when I needed you ...?"

"You needed me?" he sounded flattered.

"I wanted to introduce you to my friend Emma."

"Why?"

"Because I wanted her to see that you really do exist."

"Why?"

All these silly "why" questions! "It's because she thinks I'm just imagining you."

"Is it really that important if she believes you or not?"

"Yes."

"Why?"

"Because!"

"So you don't want to go to the sky with me?"

"No!" Angrily, Eli stomped off towards the terrace. Mrs. Meyer sat in her rocking chair drinking mint tea with strawberry flavour. Eli could smell it, surely she had not come here to just drink tea!

"Where were you yesterday?"

"Yesterday?" the old lady replied astonished. "Well, I was here."

"That's not true! I was here with Emma and no one was anywhere. And now she thinks I'm mad!"

"Yes – so what?"

"But I don't want her to think I'm mad."

"But are you? Mad, I mean."

"Of course I'm not!"

"So what's so bad about her thinking that you are, if you're not?"

Eli had the feeling she was listening to a scratched record. "I want her to finally accept that I'm right!"

"Why?"

"Can't anyone ask me a different question today?"

Mrs. Meyer put her cup down and poured more tea. "Then why did you bring her here, even though you were afraid she wasn't going to believe you?"

Eli took a sip. It was difficult to be angry whist drinking something so delicious. "I just have so much fun being with you, Nick and Luigi and I wanted Emma to see, and ... I just don't understand why she doesn't like the garden!"

"Have you ever considered the fact that not everyone thinks this garden is fun?"

"Well, she tore her socks and she got stung by the nettles."

"At least now you know that it's your garden and not hers."

"I knew that before."

"Do you know her garden?"

Eli laughed. "Emma doesn't have one at all! There's not the tiniest flower in her room or on the balcony. Not even cactuses."

"Cacti", Mrs. Meyer corrected her.

"My Grandma Augusta has some, but she only waters them if she happens not to be on a world tour. She says they grow anyway, but I think at Emma's even they would die. It doesn't make sense to bring her here again, does it?"

Mrs. Meyer shrugged. "So, what did she say?"

Eli felt her anger returning. "She said that this is not a garden, but a wilderness!"

Mrs. Meyer's wrinkles creased her forehead when she smiled. "But that's what it is. Remember, how annoyed you were about the thorny shrubs before you knew they were roses."

She poured Eli another cup of tea. "But I believe your Emma does have a garden; every person has one. They all look different of course, and the most precious flowers don't make the visitors happy, but the gardener. But it is not easy to find one and once found it is even less easy to look after it and help it to flourish."

Eli thought of Mimi and nodded.

"But however much care and effort a gardener might take, he cannot command his flowers to bloom. They have to do that by themselves. That's why his garden maybe doesn't look as beautiful and perfect as he would have planned, or hoped and longed for. But he can be sure: if the right flowers are growing there, then one day they will flower."

Eli did not really understand what Mrs. Meyer was trying to say. "Emma said that she wants to be my friend."

The wrinkles returned. "It is easy to be someone's friend if they do great things or have something fantastic to offer like talking trolls or a train that can take you to the sky. What do you think, how many admirers would you have if everyone knew? How many would want to come here and trample across the garden just to see such miracles? But all this is not important for your Emma. She doesn't like the garden and she thinks you're mad, but she still wants to be your friend. I think that her visit was extremely worthwhile."

CHAPTER ELEVEN

On Saturday, Grandma Augusta came to visit. She brought with her a suitcase and said she could not stay long, but long enough to tell Ma she should be glad to finally get rid of Pa because men are never to be trusted and anyway: she should enjoy life and not look so grumpy. Ma got quite angry after that and they fought as they always did whenever they met.

Eli spent the afternoon with Emma on her balcony and tried to imagine what type of garden her friend might have, if Mrs. Meyer was correct in that. As soon as they had finished their homework for Monday and Emma began to talk figures yet again, Eli fled.

The sun bathed the old garden in golden light and everywhere amid the roses was the scent of lavender and thyme. Mrs. Meyer had made tea which Eli enjoyed very much. After that, she lay beside Nick under the cherry tree and they watched the clouds through the tree's thinning crown – how they came together and drifted apart, how they floated, danced and drew funny and strange faces for a few seconds or minutes and for all eternity in one's memory.

Later Luigi came over and added his funny little clouds, and afterwards Eli travelled up into the evening sky with him, and Mrs. Meyer's house turned into a doll's house, and the garden into a doll's garden where Emma watered the shrubs and trees with Grandma Mary's zinc watering can. But instead of leaves and flowers, numbers and figures grew and they grew into rampant complicated maths problems in which Luigi got stuck with his waggon. Eli opened a window and looked out. Through a big fat zero she could see the pale moon and twinkling stars, and on top of a huge rainbow red cacti grew in rows of three.

When Eli got home, Grandma Augusta had unpacked her suitcase and sat silently side by side with Ma on the living room sofa.

Eli sat down in an armchair. "Tell me, Grandma: you've travelled the whole world, haven't you?"

She nodded.

"And surely you've seen some really strange things?"

"Yes, why?"

"Do you believe there may be things that can fly, but aren't rocket, balloon or aeroplane?"

"A bird", Ma said.

Grandma Augusta laughed. "You mean an airship?"

Eli beamed. "So there really are air-ships?"

"Yes, certainly. A long time ago, when I was a child, there were many of them around. Today there are only very few and they rarely take off, mainly for pleasure trips."

"And you're definitely not telling a fib?"

"But no!"

Eli gave her a big kiss on the cheek. "Thanks!"

Grandma Augusta looked moved and Ma smiled, which she never normally did when Grandma Augusta was visiting.

"How did you manage to stay married for such a long time?" Eli asked Mrs. Meyer the next time she went to the garden.

The old lady smiled. "Manage? It was wonderful being married to Otto! A little better every day."

"And you never ever wanted to separate?"

"Well, no. He loved me and his train. And I loved him and my garden."

"You never fought?"

"We did, especially when he wanted to set up his dreadful train in my beautiful garden."

"So what did you do?"

"I surrendered a little part of the lawn, which would have needed constant mowing anyway."

"But a train doesn't belong in a garden!"

Mrs. Meyer smiled. "The train was his garden. And it was not just a matter of getting used to the eccentric thing, after a while, I actu-

ally started to like it. Who else had a piece of lawn with tracks and hills and houses on it, and a train called Rudy chugging across it? At some point, Otto even started to show some interest in my half of the garden. We dug a pond, planted box bushes around the beds and roses by the pavilion and pergola." Her voice turned sombre. "And then he became sick and died, and the garden was just too large for me alone."

"But the train stayed", Eli said.

"Yes. Unfortunately you can't see it with all those nettles."

Mrs. Meyer served afternoon tea, this time with a hint of banana and ginger.

After Eli had finished, she went to look after her flowers and tomatoes. The globes, cones and bottle-shapes were already there, only the colours were still missing. She pulled-up a few weeds then went to visit Nick.

"So, what are you doing at present?"

"Nothing."

"Why do you never leave your spot?"

"Why should I?"

"Because you only ever look in the same direction!"

"It's not where I look, but what I see that's important."

"Don't you want to know what's behind the wall?"

"Why should I want to know?"

"How do you want to understand the world if you sit around all day doing nothing?"

"Why do I have to understand the world?" He said, winking. "I have to admit: my way of living might not be ideal for everyone, but it's just right for me as it is."

Eli gladly believed that, but was still not satisfied with his answer. "You're saying it doesn't matter which direction?"

"Well, yes, most of the time I like to look up anyway."

Eli had to laugh. "And up there you see those chubby cherries and wait looking forward to them falling down."

"Exactly. I then say thank you and eat them unhurriedly."

"You say thank you if a mushy cherry falls onto your head?" Eli cried amused.

"I'm thanking the cherry tree for being so kind as to let me have one. Who knows how long it is going to be able to continue to do so."

"Why?"

"The tree is very old and old trees die."

Eli thought of its lavish dress of blossom in spring, of the bulging buds from which countless leaves had grown, and of those many delicious fruits she had harvested, and the many she saw still left on the branches.

"That's a lie."

"Everyone has to die one day."

"I know that!"

But actually, Eli had never really thought about it: dying. Grandma Mary had always worked in the garden, planted flowers and vegetables, weeded, picked berries, made jam – but one day she was just not there anymore. Actually, she was still there, but she lay on her bed pale and silent and wore a white lace nightdress with her hands folded. And a blue cloth wrapped around her chin which looked a bit strange. Then she had gone from the bed too, and everyone had listened to the vicar, and Eli had been terribly cold in the churchyard, and had wondered what that hole in the ground had to do with Grandma Mary's new home in heaven.

Eli had promised God, she would drink a glass of black currant juice every day for a whole year, if he would only send Grandma Mary back, but it was obviously not sacrifice enough in God's view.

Eli doubted that what everyone said was true: if Grandma Mary, and all the others that had died, actually lived in heaven and if there was a heavenly garden like Pa said, why had she never noticed it during her trips with Luigi? And when she watched the clouds with Nick, there seemed nothing to suggest that anyone lived up there, except the sun, moon and the stars. And the rainbow, of course. Well, and maybe the wind, if it didn`t happen to be in the Tower of Winds at the time and perhaps the snow in winter, if it did not happen to be falling to Earth bringing a little colour to the snowdrops. Not even Grandpa Friedhelm could keep Grandma Mary company as he had fallen in the war, whatever that might mean. But if trees died: did

they continue growing in the heavenly garden if it actually existed somewhere? But how were they supposed to get there?

"You can't really know that the tree is dying because only half of it is visible!" Eli said.

Nick yawned vigorously. "Maybe that's exactly why I know: because I can see the half that matters."

Eli could feel the awful lump growing in her throat again. "You don't know. You just think you know!"

It was a pathetic try, to make this horrible statement unsaid. "Anyway: what are you going to do if you don't have a trunk to lean to?"

The troll straightened his pointed cap.

"Firstly, I don't know if I will still be around when the trunk has gone. Secondly, I'm fine. I have a great time. Why should I spoil everything with thoughts on what might be if things weren't so wonderful anymore? Particularly, because I won't be able to change anything anyway. Maybe in the end everything is different, but just wonderfully different and then the thoughts would have been in vein and I will have wasted precious hours."

"That's not a sensible answer!"

"Does every question need a sensible answer?"

"When is the cherry tree going to die?"

"Don't know."

"But if you know that it's going to die, then you must also know when!"

"The flowers die every year."

"That's something different."

"Why?"

Eli tried to fight the lump. "Because ... You're daft!" And before he could reply, she ran away.

Mrs. Meyer had put the tea things away and was reading a thick book. Breathless, Eli let herself drop into a wicker chair. "Can you tell me what it's like when one dies?"

"Why do you want to know?" asked the old lady astonished.

"Nick says the cherry tree is dying. But Pa says trees live for a very long time."

"It depends on the tree. A beech can live for up to three hundred, an oak even up to a thousand years. Trees like the cherry that bear fruit for many years, don't usually live as long. Besides, they can become sick just like human beings and die much earlier."

"But it looks so alive!"

Mrs. Meyer put her book aside and together they went over to the cherry tree. Eli stopped in front of the trunk so Nick couldn't see them. Mrs. Meyer pointed to the thinning crown. "The bark is coming off. And the shiny bit beside it is resin. People say: the tree is bleeding."

Yes, Eli could see it. And if she looked carefully, she saw even more: bare branches between green leaves and red cherries. Further up, a big branch pointed towards the sky and it did not have a single leaf. Why had she not noticed that before?

"How long is it going to live?" she sadly asked.

Mrs. Meyer shrugged. "For years it has had less and less leaves, flowers and fruit. Also it grows almost no fresh wood. But it's still here."

Eli nodded, but the lump did not go away. No matter how many more years the old tree was going to survive: she would never be able to look at it and feel overpowering happiness again. From now on, there would always be a touch of melancholy, a hint of autumn, even in mid-summer. She searched for comfort at the pond and when she saw funny Luigi rumbling across the roots with his rusty red minicarriage, she immediately felt better.

"I'm on my way up to the sky. Coming along?" he asked and opened a door.

Eli nodded, climbed in and sat by the window. She pulled back the curtains and, as always, all small things turned large: blades of grass swayed in the wind like reeds, daisies turned into giant marguerites and the larkspur flowers looked like blue soup dishes with a blob of cream. Unabashed, Luigi rattled across the orange reddish shaggy heads of the marigolds and almost got stuck in a carpet of rosé coloured rose petals. He slalomed along a seemingly never ending blackberry creeper between thorns the size of daggers and headed for the cherry tree. Eli definitely did not want to go there now! But no matter how much she waved and shouted, Luigi resolutely kept going.

"Something wrong?" he asked when they had reached the tree, luckily on the opposite side from Nick.

"I don't know if I want to go up there today", Eli said.

"I thought you liked the old fellow?"

"Nick and Mrs. Meyer say that it's going to die soon."

Luigi let off a little cloud of good temper. "What a load of twaddle! Something with a trunk like that isn't going to die any time soon." He dived into the ivy and swerved his way upwards. "Did you know lots of animals that live here wouldn't be around if this was a young tree? Look how much life there is everywhere!"

Indeed: giant beetles and spiders of the same proportion were crawling along, and huge ants were drumming on ball-sized greenfly. Eli noticed an abandoned blackbird's nest as large as a haystack. And a dragonfly, so majestic and iridescently beautiful as if it had swallowed all the colours of the rainbow. They stopped at the place to which Mrs. Meyer had pointed previously.

Gleaming and hard, the resin stuck to the bark.

"Tree gold", Luigi remarked.

"Mrs. Meyer says the tree is bleeding", Eli replied.

Luigi laughed. "Does that look like blood to you?"

Eli shook her head. The colour reminded her of honey and the precious necklace Pa had given Ma when they had still celebrated Christmas together. Amber he had called it. Luigi pointed to bluish-green rosettes, flat as pancakes, which grew all over the bark. "Those are magic cherry tree stars."

Now Eli laughed too, because she knew exactly that this was lichen which always grows on the bark of old trees. Pa had once explained this to her and it was also mentioned in her clever book. But she had never realised how pretty it could look. Luigi continued and the smell of resin and warm wood accompanied them. Finally they reached the bare skyward branch and Luigi let off two clouds of smoke.

"Isn't this a marvellous view?"

"The branch is dead", Eli said.

"If there were leaves on it, we wouldn't be able to see as much. Look at all those magic stars!"

"It's lichen."

Eli thought she heard a sigh. But since when did trains sigh?

She noticed something luminous between the twists of ivy and Luigi went closer. "Ah!" he said happily. "That's where their houses are."

"Those aren't houses, that's tree fungi", instructed Eli. She knew this particularly well, because Pa had shown her some during one of their raids through Matt's Wood and had emphasised that it only grew on sick or dead trees.

"Don't you know where the fairies live?" Luigi asked.

"What fairies?"

"Are you really telling me you run around the garden at night and have not heard, seen or at least felt them?"

"I don't run around the garden at night."

"Oh dear – you've missed half your life! Anyway, those are the houses of fairies and that's why this tree is surely not going to die. That's because it's a fairy-ivy-tree."

"But ..."

"I swear solemnly three times over. Cross my heart and hope to die!"

Eli had to laugh again and Luigi sounded off his funny toot and then they travelled straight into the midst of the yelloworangered-purple sunset sky.

It was already dark when they returned to the garden. The pond was like a black sea, the stream had turned into a rapid river, and the pavilion was a silhouette the size of a temple. It crickled and crackled and rustled and bustled and the frogs' croaks were in minor, the chirping of the cicadas in major in the orchestra of the night. Suddenly the ensemble was interrupted by dissonant huffing.

"Oh dear", Luigi said. "It's the hedgehogs."

"The hedgehogs?" Eli asked astonished. "It sounds more like a bricklayer carrying heavy stones, at least as if they are really straining themselves."

"In truth: they are." Luigi sounded amused. That is if rusty trains, that are really airships, are able to sound amused.

They continued on their way. The wind whispered through the bamboo and the night composed a new song of it.

"I like to be on the move at night", Luigi said.

"As a ship?" Eli asked.

"Well, sometimes it's quite useful to pretend to be a train."

"Ah", said Eli, trying hard to supress a laugh. Then a delicate aroma found her nose. "Where does that come from?"

"There are flowers you can only smell in the dark", Luigi said. "Just like the fairies' perfume. If you are very quiet you will see them dance."

"See them dance? The fairies? Me?"

"Yes. But we have to be very, very quiet."

A mouse the size of a pig crossed their path, whimpering, and they were so shocked they almost collided with a salad bowl-sized snail. On the top of a crumbly mount of soil a huge rosy earthworm wiggled and man-sized bats did their rounds near the ancient lilac bush.

"I used to think everyone was asleep at this time", Eli said.

"Not everyone's like you", Luigi replied.

That almost sounded as if it came from Nick. The thought amused Eli. How silly she had been, being furious at a lazy stone troll! The cherry tree was alive and it was summer.

"Well, let's see if your fairies are at home then."

But wherever they were, Eli did not see the fairies that night.

CHAPTER TWELVE

"Eli! Wake up!" Ma called from the door and for a change she did not have to call twice. Eli leapt out of bed and ran to the window. When she saw the empty space where Mimi had been, she was sad. But then she looked up to the sky and the good mood returned: a sunny summer's morning and finally the last school day before the holidays was here!

Eli's report was not particularly good nor was it particularly bad, but anyway, she had other things to worry about than her school marks. Emma had been praised for being the best pupil in the class. Although this was nothing new, behind her glasses her eyes sparkled and her cheeks blushed bright red with delight.

„Little swat", one girl hissed when Emma walked past.

„Leave her alone, will you!" Eli snapped.

The girl laughed contemptuously. "Are you friends with that boring nerd?"

"Yes, actually I am. She's my friend – just so you know!" Eli said this loud enough so all the others would hear. She linked arms with Emma and they paraded out of the classroom.

"That'll teach them, won't it?" she said on the way home.

Emma stopped and looked at hear doubtfully. "Are we really proper friends? Even if we quarrel sometimes?"

Eli smiled. "Of course."

Emma's eyes started filling up again. "That's even better than my school report!"

Suddenly, Eli felt light and elated. She took Emma's hand and they skipped and sang and fooled around until they reached their street. There was a sign outside the flower lady's shop. *Closed!*

"*Business closing down*", Emma said, reading the rest aloud.

This could not be true! Eli knocked on the door and tried to get a look inside through the stickered window.

"No one's there anymore", Emma said. "Come on, let's go."

Eli kept knocking. She heard steps, then the door being unlocked.

The flower lady was wearing a blue blouse and had clean hands. She greeted them with a smile.

"Why did you close down your shop?" Eli asked.

"Not enough customers."

"But you have such beautiful flowers!"

"Prices are lower in the city."

"Then lower your prices, too!"

"My shop's too small."

"Then make it bigger!"

"It's not that easy."

"And where am I now supposed to get the flowers for my rainbow bed from?"

"Didn't you tell me it was finished a while ago?"

"Yes, right. But I will surely want to plant another one soon."

The flower lady smiled. "Well, then come with me. I have something really pretty for you. And something for your friend, too, if she likes."

When she heard the word friend, Emma's cheeks started to blush bright red. They followed the flower lady into the empty shop. She asked them to wait, whilst she went into the next room and came back with two little flower pots, one white, the other one red. Inside the white one, a red flower was blossoming and a white one in the red pot. The flowers looked interesting: delicate and fragile; and a little mischievous. "These are called Busy Lizzies", the flower lady said. "They flower all year round, in the garden or on the balcony during the summer and on the windowsill in winter." She looked at Eli and added. "If one doesn't forget to water them."

Eli nodded and took the white pot, Emma hesitantly took the red one. "Thank you", she said politely.

Eli grinned. Emma and flowers! How long was the poor Busy Lizzie going to be busy with her? "If you don't really want it you can give it to me", Eli said a bit patronisingly.

Emma shook her head. "No, it's pretty. I'll keep it." And then they proceeded to bombard the flower lady with questions: if one should nip off the dead blossoms and how often, when and how much one was supposed to water the Lizzie and if she preferred the sun or shade.

"In the shade", the flower lady said. "And if at some point she stops flowering, just pinch off a few new shoots and put them in water. As soon as they have grown roots, you put them back into soil and – voilá – you've got Baby Lizzies."

"Really?" Emma blurted out enthusiastically. The flower lady nodded.

"Are you never going to sell flowers again?" Eli asked.

"I have sold flowers all my life. At some point it had to come to an end."

"So, what are you going to do now?"

"Move to the countryside, go for walks, read books and enjoy the summer. How's your lucky clover doing?"

Eli realised she was blushing with embarrassment. "Well, it's fine."

The flower lady wrapped the Lizzies up in newspaper. Emma took her package with an expression on her face as if it was a treasure chest full of diamonds.

"The clover needs light and water", the flower lady said and Eli nodded.

"Today's a wonderful day!" Emma rejoiced when they were back in the street.

Eli did not say anything. She would never have believed that the day the flower lady closed her shop for good could ever be a wonderful day.

As usual, Ma was not there when Eli got home. She dropped her school bag in the hall, went to her room and unwrapped Lizzie and put it in Mimi's place. Then she found the yoghurt pot with the lucky clover from her night table. Two pale stalks sprouted from the bone-dry soil. They looked pitiful.

Eli held the pot under the tap and then put it back onto the windowsill. She was sure: they were not going to make it. But the day was far too sunny to be sad about anything and the cherry tree looked so tempting. Also, she really felt like some strawberry flavoured mint tea.

Mrs. Meyer sat in her rocking chair; in her lap she had a tray lined with paper and a wicker basket with sunny yellow and orange flowers.

"What are you doing?" Eli asked.

"I'm drying marigolds. For tea and creams."

"Oh yes, right", Eli remembered. "Grandma Mary used to do the same, too. And she also used to laugh about the silly people who spent lots of money on creams at the pharmacy although everything grows in the garden for free. Just because they didn't have a clue or the time and were far too lazy." Eli sighed. "My Ma doesn't have time. And Pa doesn't anymore either. And Grandma Augusta has none at all."

Mrs. Meyer took a yellow marigold bloom and plucked the petals off onto a tray. "Although, actually it's really easy."

"What?"

"To give yourself a little time."

"And how?"

"Well, you should better go and ask the expert."

Eli ran over to the cherry tree. "Good afternoon, Nick! Can you tell me how one gives oneself time?"

The troll was contemplating some white flowers that looked like a cross between daisies and fabric covered buttons.

"Look, how many petals these have and how the sun makes them shine!" Eli started to say something, but he shook his head. "Go and touch them. They smell of camomile."

"Brrr! I always had to drink camomile tea when I've had tummy-ache."

"It's not tea, but a lawn, and it's made of honey. You will smell it as soon as you walk across it."

Until now, Eli had not been particularly interested in the green carpet that stretched out near the ferns, but with those white buttons on it, it looked quite pretty. Nick was right: wherever she set foot, it smelled camomile-honey-sweet – and then she actually discovered some wild strawberries! Amidst the white of the camomile, they almost seemed like little puckered lips and Eli picked all she could find. A ladybird crawled across her hand and a furry bumble bee flew into a purple blue bell, humming away. Powdered all over with pollen, it

emerged and disappeared into the next one. A slowworm wound its way through the grass and below a mossy stone two fire salamanders were hiding. The sparrows chatted away in the bushes. When Eli had finished nibbling, she was surprised to see she had wandered all the way to the bamboo.

"Sorry", she said when she got back to Nick. "With all those strawberries around, I totally forgot about the time."

"You gave yourself the time", the troll said.

"I dawdled around!"

Nick smiled. "*Dawdle* – I like that. You have dawdled an hour of time for yourself. Isn't that wonderful?"

Laughing, Eli ran towards the terrace. Mrs. Meyer had finished plucking the marigolds. Eli sat down. "I would never have thought that an hour could be so short and long at the same time!"

The old lady smiled and her wrinkles turned into funny little ripples on her forehead. "You can have some time for yourself everywhere, but it is especially easy in a garden: a second, that a dewdrop needs to run off a leaf or a bird needs to land on a branch; a minute, that's how long his song lasts; the hour, early or late, when the blossom opens and closes again – there are so many precious moments every day, week or month in which plants grow, linger and die. In a garden you can turn seconds into minutes, an hour into a day and one day into a whole life. Or a whole life turns into a single day. I've made tea, would you like some?"

To her surprise Eli saw Emma standing near the wall the next morning. She had brought a basket and was smiling sheepishly. "I thought it might be nice to have a little picnic in your enchanted garden."

And from that moment on, some wonderful days began and they passed more quickly than Eli could have ever believed. Unfortunately, neither Mrs. Meyer nor Luigi ever showed themselves whilst she was there with Emma, and Nick persistently refused to say a word, but Eli and Emma had fun together anyway.

They picked sugar-sweet raspberries and sour-sweet blackberries, nibbled red, white and even some black currants; they rubbed fragrant herbs between their hands, picked flowers in the meadow and

tasted the first mini tomatoes. Emma brought two cups, sugar and a thermos flask of hot water and they had a different sort of mint tea every day. At some point they even hauled over a bucket, detergent, cleaning rags and a brush and cleaned the house. Eli had to admit that up until now she had not noticed the dirt and dust and masses of cobwebs. Obviously, neither had Mrs. Meyer.

Eli felt it was a great pity that she did not succeed in having all her friends with her simultaneously, but after a while she just came to terms with it. Emma often brought her books along and Eli was surprised at how easy it seemed for her to read for hours on end or just sit there thinking. She began to envy Emma: she had obviously already perfected the art of niggling extra time for oneself. Whilst Emma was busy with her books, she did not forget two things: lunch and her Busy Lizzie which she looked after with such dedication, of which Eli had never thought her capable.

Soon, half the summer holidays had passed. For the final two weeks, Pa invited Eli to join himself and Kate for a trip to the Baltic Sea. Eli had looked forward to the sand and sea in spite of Kate, but also especially to spending more time with Pa. As it turned out, she would have actually preferred to stay in the garden with Emma.

On the evening prior to the trip, she carried her red Lizzie together with the pot of sad lucky clover over to Emma's for safe keeping. Then she went to the garden to say goodbye to Mrs. Meyer, Nick and Luigi. "I would like to show you something", Mrs. Meyer by way of a greeting.

Curious, Eli followed her to the shed behind the house where the pot with the dead olive was, and it took her a moment to realise that there were silvery-green leaves growing from the stump she had so radically mutilated in spring.

Mrs. Meyer smiled. "Thanks to your artistic way of pruning, my olive tree now has to spend its second life as a bush." They laughed and Eli thought of Luigi's twisted little box which still lay at the back of her desk. Since Christmas, it must have been filled with so many wonderful *Tomorrows* that it was probably full to bursting by now.

After saying her goodbyes to Nick and Luigi, Eli drank a farewell cup of tea with Mrs. Meyer out on the terrace. The old lady gave her a

thin little book that had a little boy in green trousers and golden hair on the front. "It's the story of the little prince", she said. "I think the time is now right to tell you how it all ends."

And then she told her how the little prince had left his tiny garden and his beautiful rose and travelled far and wide and finally fell to Earth. And of his disappointment in discovering that his rose was not unique at all, but grew in thousands of gardens. And how he found two friends, a sly fox and a crashed pilot, who then helped him to appreciate that his rose was actually unique after all. Because it was his rose.

"And although the little prince had taken a liking to both fox and pilot, he was forced to leave them because his visiting time on Earth had come to an end. And so it was that he returned to his garden and to his rose. His friends, however, still keep him in fond memory."

"That's a very sad story", Eli said.

Mrs. Meyer shook her head. "Visits always come to an end at some point, but saying goodbye is a lot easier if the hours spent together were fulfilling, and one feels comfortably content and pleasantly tired after a long day. And if you are not forgotten by the ones you love." Eli still felt the story was sad.

"Things can be taken from you", the old lady continued. "But not your feelings", she smiled and her wrinkles looked sad and happy at the same time. "You have planted your flowers and just as the little prince, the memories will keep your yearning alive. One day you will find your garden again. And all the flowers will be in bloom."

"I'm sure they will!" Eli said laughing and shook her hand. "Take care and look after Nick and Luigi. I will be back in two weeks' time!"

Eli had intended to be nice to Kate, but it was difficult for her. To be fair, Kate was really quite nice and it was probably difficult for her too. The sea was wonderful, as was the beach, and Kate allowed her and Pa lots of time together. Still, nothing was as it had been and it wasn't any fault of Kate's, but that of the old garden. After just one day Eli was already missing it, and the delicious tea, and Mrs. Meyer, Nick and Luigi - even Emma! Pa built a giant Matt's Fort with her in the sand and they frolicked in the water and laughed and he called

her Ronia, even though she would have preferred him to continue calling her Eli. He was not a robber chieftain any longer, he was Pa and he had a belly and pale legs and Eli had grown-up and the dark forest had long turned into a secret garden. In the evening whilst lying in bed, she tried to imagine what things would be like when she returned. All the tomatoes would be ripe, even the tall crooked ones. The marigolds would still be in flower, but not the camomile, unfortunately. And apple fragrance would fill the air and the leaves would soon be turning colourful. She would be seeing the garden in its glorious autumn dress for a second time, but this year she would enjoy it from the beginning.

The time at the seaside passed more quickly than Eli had thought and by the end she had even got used to Kate. The day before the last was her birthday. Pa gave her a new cassette player and Kate let them have the whole day to themselves to celebrate. No, it was not Kate's fault that Ma and Pa were not going to get back together; her presence just confirmed it. Eli realised that the thought of it did not hurt anymore. Mrs. Meyer's garden helped her in that respect too.

They returned home on a Friday in late summer, just right for visiting Mrs. Meyer for an hour to say hello. It was loud and dusty in the street and there was no grass left on the piece of land in front of the wall. Earth and stones formed a greyish-brown heap that was being shovelled onto a lorry by a digger. Eli gasped: the wall was gone! Pa had not even managed to bring the car to a complete halt before she jumped out. She ran and stumbled, madly oblivious, over junk and stones to the place where the gap in the wall had been. But she did not need it anymore, because now you could enter the garden from everywhere.

Mrs. Meyer's house had no roof, no windows, doors and no terrace, no stairs and no rocking chair any more. The digger tracks gouged scars straight across the middle of Eli's rainbow bed, through the meadow and mint over to where the bamboo had been. Eli searched for the little stream and pond and for the pavilion but only crushed, naked earth was left. The camomile lawn and the strawberries had gone, the bamboo greens, rose stems and branches were piled head-high. Eli buried her face in her hands in horror. She did not want to see it! Sawdust on the ground, a fresh tree stump with torn ivy tendrils beside it.

"Nick!" she called out desperately. "Luigi! Where are you?"

Somebody was talking to her. Good natured, dusty faces of workers; even the digger driver had clambered out. "You can't wander around here, little girl. It's too dangerous!"

"Why did you destroy everything? Why?"

Suddenly, Pa was beside her. He stroked her hair but she did not even feel it. She wanted to get to the old house and look for Mrs. Meyer, but he would not let her. She started to strike-out viciously, crying and screaming until all her strength finally left her and Pa carried her home.

Later on, Emma came up and sat by her bedside. "But look: we still have our Lizzies."

"Yes", Eli said. "And a pot full of dried lucky clover."

"Nope", Emma said. "It's growing again."

Eli cried and Emma joined in making things feel a little better.

When Eli finally awoke it was dark. She could hear Ma and Pa talking in the living room. No, actually not talking! They were quarrelling again. Eli would have loved to block the sound from her ears. She got up and opened the window. Autumn fragrance was in the air. By the pale light of the street lamps, the digger turned into a grey and black monster. The voices next door got louder. Eli closed the window and crept into the corridor.

"With all those fairy tales you keep telling the child, it's no surprise that she flees into a fantasy world of her own!" Ma shouted.

"So she went secretly to the overgrown garden and enjoyed being there. So what?" Pa said. Eli wanted to kiss him for that. He still was her brave robber chieftain – just a little.

"She must continue her therapy!" Ma said.

Eli burst in. "I don't need therapy. I need parents that will finally stop shouting at each other."

Mum and Pa looked full of remorse and Eli felt quite grown up. Without another word she returned to her room.

When she awoke for the second time, drawn was already breaking. Quietly, she got dressed and left the flat. Outside it was calm and cool; thin wispy fog lay across the barren piece of land, earth and rubble were heaped in magic hills and pink clouds drifted across the sky. *Red sky in the morning, shepherd's warning,* Grandma Mary had always said.

The garden, or what was left of it, lay defenceless and vulnerable before her, but this time Eli was prepared for it. Quietly, she called for Nick and Luigi, but they were gone. Nothing was left of her rainbow bed. Beneath the shattered planks she found a handful of bent marigolds and Mrs. Meyer's broken rocking chair. The colourful tomatoes, which she had so been looking forward to, had all been torn out and smashed. Eli went around the house. Nothing of the things she had so loved was left: the funny ferns from the flower lady, the resurrected olive tree, the witch-hazel and the pergola, Luigi's root, not even the blackberries and stinging nettles were left. It was just as if there had never been an old garden.

Eli sat on the sawdust-covered stump that had been the cherry tree. Something lay in the grass in front of her. She picked it up. It was the rusty chimney of a toy train.

The sun climbed into the sky. Everywhere there were broken branches, wilted leaves clinging limply to the injured wood where also next year's bud-children could be clearly seen. Fractured pieces of bark with lichen. A smatter of tree blood, congealed and sticky. Eli wiped her eyes. Nick had known. That was why he had told her about dying: to make the farewell easier for her. Suddenly, she had the feeling he was sitting behind her. She did not dare turn around for fear of it being just a figment of her imagination, wishful thinking.

"I couldn't stay here. You understand that now, don't you?"

"Where are you living nowadays?"

"I'm there where Luigi also lives."

"But the root has gone!" Eli turned round but Nick had disappeared.

Two women went past in the street. "It was about time they tore down that ramshackle hut", one of them said.

"Yes. Just look at that massive pile of junk! The seeds from all those weeds were constantly being blown over the wall into my garden."

They stopped and looked in Eli's direction, but did not seem to notice her. "They say the town bought the plot. They want to build a nursery school."

"It has taken long enough for the old lady's heirs to finally agree. It was quite a tragedy really."

The second woman nodded and they continued on their way.

Heirs? What Heirs? Eli crept round the remains of the old house. Nick had been here! But now he didn't speak to her any more. Instead, she could hear the familiar sound of a funny toot and saw a tiny white cloud rising from a pile of branches. The branch-piles suddenly disappeared and the old garden was back the way it was and what she saw was truly real. How could it have been any different? She thought of Pa. Had she not just realised that he had left, but was not actually gone? It was just that the path to him was now different. And this path had taken her into Mrs. Meyer's garden.

The house looked like a large dead animal. It was murky inside. Eli's eyes slowly got used to the dim light. The furniture was gone and a thick layer of dust was everywhere. Eli sat down on the stove bench and touched the cracked tiles. How happy she had been here! She closed her eyes. *And soon here, soon there, whispering voices arose asking "Isn't she coming yet?" and others replied: "Not yet, but soon." And then it was midday, a hot, blazing midday and silence descended, a deep, expectant silence. But this hour also passed without the old lady appearing.*

Eli opened her eyes as someone sat down beside her and she saw she was back in the garden. Pa had come. In his hand he held the book of the little prince with green trousers and golden hair.

"Where did you get that from?" she asked surprised.

"It was in the house beside the stove."

"Mrs. Meyer told me the story, but I didn't understand it all."

"It's a fairy tale", Pa said. "Similar to the one about Ronia. Similar the one about the old garden." He stroked her cheek caringly "You know, there comes a time when those stories are no longer true. That's when you're grown-up."

"But they were always true for you!"

"Because you were there for me to tell them." He said, looking at her seriously. Eli took his hand. "Don't worry, Pa. I don't believe in Father Christmas anymore."

He smiled; Eli looked over to the old house. In one of the black holes of a window stood Mrs. Meyer, waving.

And the warm breeze of transience was within her and with the clear, cold breath of the stars everything was complete, death and life. "It's for the best", the old lady murmured. And as the light from the room fell across her face, everyone in the garden could see that her tears had dried. Eli nodded in her direction and got up.

"I think, now the time is right to leave."

WE DON'T SEE THE THINGS
THE WAY THEY ARE,
WE SEE THEM,
THE WAY WE ARE.

from the Talmud

Se non è vero, è molto ben trovato.
If it is not true, it is very well invented.

Giordano Bruno

Epilogue

"So, what's that ramshackle hut supposed to cost?" The woman wore a thick layer of make-up, around her mid-forties and so slim, it almost hurt. The estate agent repeated the price. The woman laughed piercingly. "I would hope that includes the waste disposal skips for the disposal of all that", she said, pointing at the remains of the overgrown garden, "heaps of weeds!"

„That's something you need to talk the owner about, madam. Would you like to take a look at the house now?"

"If you tell me where it is?" came the answer, sarcastically.

"Well, it's not very large but ..."

"Can we add an extension?"

The estate agent beamed. "Of course! If you like, I can show you the development plans."

"I'd prefer you to show me the entrance!"

The estate agent glanced at Marcus. "In the meantime, maybe you and your wife would like to have a look around out here?"

Marcus nodded. "We have time."

"Well I haven't!" the woman exclaimed. She stumbled off towards the house which had almost completely disappeared behind a wall of ivy. The estate agent followed her.

"Wonderful!" Eli enthused when they were out of earshot. "But did you hear the price? Far too expensive for us."

Marcus kissed the tip of her nose. He always did that if he was up to something. "I have a slight suspicion that they can maybe do something about the price."

Eli looked to the door which was just closing behind the lady and the estate agent. "And I have a slight suspicion she has more to offer than we have."

Marcus smirked. "If she was as well situated as she pretends, she would be looking at a villa with a pool instead of a housing estate in the suburbs that has seen better days." Eli laughed and linked arms with Marcus. They walked along the narrow path that led between the house and the garage into the back garden. The plot was not particularly large, but densely overgrown and surrounded by a wall. Autumn had already coloured the bushes brightly, making the green of the ivy appear particularly intense.

"We would have to cut it back a little", Marcus said.

"You just leave that to me, will you", Eli replied.

"Yes, yes: the house is mine, the garden's yours."

"Exactly! And that's that ..." She stared at the tree, its foliage shining brightly in multitude shades of yellow. Ivy climbed the trunk all the way up to the sparse crown. Around a weathered tree bench shone lush green fronds of fern. "This can't be true."

"What can't?" Marcus asked.

Eli sat down on the bench. Hops and ivy were growing through it and had woven themselves into two-tone green dress. She gazed up to where the main branches forked and greyish blue lichen covered the cracked bark.

"I don't believe it!"

Marcus sat down beside her. "I presume you like the garden", he said with a smile. Like? That was much too weak a way to express it. Eli could scent the earthy hint of transience and it brought back memories, the pain, the tears, the grief, but also comfort and happiness, spring, summer, abundance, colours. And a cherry tree in the middle. A childhood dream.

"I need to call Emma right now!"

"Didn't you say she's in New York?"

Eli nodded and got out her mobile phone. "I'm going to text her." She punched: *Found my garden. The house is ok, too *LOL*. Look forward to seeing you soon. Eli*

"Oh, here you are!"

With his dark suit and his neatly parted hair the estate agent looked out of place. Judging by the attentiveness with which he suddenly turned towards them, despite them not exactly being his prefer-

red clientele, the other lady had not been that interested. Eli's heart leaped. Maybe there was a possibility to discuss the price again? Her thought was barely finished when her hopes were shattered. The lady pranced towards them from the garage, behaving as though Eli and Marcus didn't exist.

"If you make sure all this scrub", she pointed to the ivy coat of the house, the bushes in front of the wall and the old cherry tree, "disappears immediately, I might give the whole thing a second thought." She shrugged, "After all, I'm not going to move in myself."

A new glimpse of hope. "You're intending to rent it out?" Eli asked.

The lady gave her a disdainful look. "No. My daughter needs a decent place. She's studying at university and definitely doesn't have the time to look after this wilderness!" She turned towards the agent again: "You said you know a landscape gardener?"

"No!" Eli shouted.

Agent and lady stared at her as if she had suddenly turned into Dracula. Even Marcus looked slightly irritated. Eli could tell by the expression on his face that he had given up hope of a price reduction, but Eli was sure that a lucky coincidence had brought them here and she really wanted this house. No, it was more than that: she just had to have this garden!

"You don't have to trouble the landscape gardener. We will buy the house as is."

She saw that Marcus definitely doubted her sanity. The lady, however, seemed to get into the fighting spirit.

"I just said that I am prepared ..."

"May I invite you for a cup of coffee?"

Without them noticing, an old man had joined the company. He had snow-white hair, wore a patched cardigan and trousers that were far too big. He took Eli's hand and feigned a kiss.

"Meyer's my name. I'm very happy to welcome you to my home."

"Mr. Meyer, please!" the agent said. It was obvious that he was becoming less than happy.

"You said you didn't want coffee", Mr. Meyer replied.

Eli stood transfixed. "Is your name really Meyer?"

The agent looked at her as if he, too, was beginning to doubt her sanity. The old man smiled. "I suppose there are quite a few people around in this country with that name, isn't that so?"

This really could not be coincidence anymore! Alright, the garden was smaller and the house not quite as old, but the cherry tree ... Eli bent down to look underneath the bench. Nothing. Of course. What had she expected? She was behaving like a silly little girl! They would never be able to afford this house, in the middle of an urban centre. A house that needed a lot of work doing to it and anyway, the lady would surely outbid them.

"Thank you for your kind offer, Mr. Meyer. I'd love to have a cup of coffee with you."

Mr. Meyer beamed. The agent rolled his eyes.

The lady pulled out a business card and handed it to the agent. "I have made my offer and await your call tomorrow morning at the latest."

The agent nodded and the lady left.

"Is there any chance of discussing the price?" Marcus asked.

"No", said the agent.

"It depends", said Mr. Meyer.

The agent turned towards Marcus. "I have another appointment, if you'll excuse me. Should you wish to buy, please make sure you call me today." Throwing an angry glance over to Mr. Meyer, he left.

Eli and Marcus followed Mr. Meyer into the house. It was very small indeed, but for the student daughter of a wealthy mother it was actually not too bad, especially since she seemed to have the wherewithal to employ armies of workmen before moving in. She and Marcus, however, did not even have the necessary means to pay the asking price!

Mr. Meyer asked them into the living room, it was comfortable with a very dark wooden floor and – something that did not surprise Eli - a meadow-green tiled stove, which was spreading cosy warmth. The wallpaper had turned yellow and was out of fashion, the carpet threadbare. But the furniture was beautiful, made of walnut, and was surely older than the house itself.

Mr. Meyer pointed to a sofa and two armchairs and asked them to have a seat. He disappeared into the adjoining room, presumably the

kitchen. They could hear him pottering about and then caught the aroma of freshly ground coffee.

Mr. Meyer came back with a tray laden with cups, plates, sugar, milk and a bowl of chocolate biscuits. "It seems I almost sensed I would be sharing my coffee with someone else today." Smiling broadly, he put the biscuits and crockery onto the table and went to fetch the coffee. "Hand brewed", he said proudly. That reminded Eli of Grandma Mary and anyway, she seemed to have slipped into a totally different time-zone since entering the garden.

"So, where's your wife?" she asked and promptly received a disgusted look from Marcus. She knew such questions were impolite as, at his age, there were not too many alternatives, but she just could not help herself.

And, sure enough, the sad reply came: "My Millie died a long time ago." Millie – a pet name for Emily? Or Mildred! Had old Mrs. Meyer not told her on her first visit to call her auntie Mildred? Despite the heat of the stove, Eli felt her blood run cold. "You must surely have been married for a long time?"

"Oh yes, we ..."

Marcus spluttered his coffee and started to cough. Mr. Meyer patted him on the back which made him cough even more. "Thanks, thanks a lot!" he said, waving him away whilst cutting Eli a furious look.

"We don't want to keep you much longer", he said when he could finally breathe again. "And I will be honest with you: we can't afford to pay you the asking price. My wife's remark was, well, a little premature."

Eli could smell the strawberry mint and she could hear the blackbirds sing and the cherries tasted of summer and yearning. Well, that was the end of it! There was no sense in longing after childish dreams.

"My husband's right."

"But why then did you say you wanted to buy the house?"

He did not sound disappointed, not angry, not even surprised; just curious. He smiled with his wrinkles, just as Mrs. Meyer had done.

"It may sound strange", Eli answered a little embarrassed. "But I fell in love with your garden immediately. Because ..." She did not know how to explain the inexplicable, but he looked at her in such a friendly and patient way that she found the courage. "It's your cherry tree. I have loved cherries since my childhood."

"Me too. Especially the stones!" he said mischievously. "That old chap has been growing out there for many decades. He's even older than the house and me." And then he suddenly became serious. "He's probably not going to last very much longer."

"Surely at least another few summers", Eli replied. "And then he will turn into a fairy-ivy-tree where the blackbirds can build their nests. I would love to make a little stream and a pond in its shade, with frogs and elves. Don't you think that the lichen on the branches look like magic stars? And those ferns around it ... Well, your garden's just magical!"

Marcus' expression revealed that he was wondering who exactly this woman sitting opposite him was.

Eli was embarrassed. How on earth could she talk such nonsense! What would Mr. Meyer think of her? If she were in his shoes, she would definitely not sell the house to herself – especially not if she was seriously concerned about seeing money at some point.

Mr. Meyer topped-up her coffee. "My son commissioned the agent. He constantly brings in people I don't like: people trample through with thoughts of how quickly the house can be cleared, wanting to plough the garden and cut down all the trees. People who want to put on extensions or make conversions, who find my wallpaper old-fashioned and complain about the cracked tiles on my stove. People who think the ceilings are too light, the wooden floors too dark and the furniture not old enough to fetch a good price at the antiques dealer."

"Your furniture is beautiful", Eli said.

"My son believes he has the right to do all this. Well, he doesn't. Yes, I have told him I will go into a home. But I still reserve the right to decide who is going to move into my house and to whom I will give my garden."

"We don't have enough money ...", Marcus started.

"Everything I am going to need for the rest of my life, I have already." Mr. Meyer looked at Eli. "When I was a little lad, I lived in an old house and, as the story went, there was treasure hidden somewhere inside. Of course, no one was ever able to discover it, but maybe that was because no one ever really looked for it. But it put a spell on the whole house. My house had a deep secret at the bottom of its heart."

"Yes", Eli said. *"It matters not if it is house or desert – the source of its beauty is invisible."*

They laughed and Marcus looked confused.

"The little Prince", Mr. Meyer explained, "was my late wife's favourite book." He turned towards Eli. "My Millie always said it was the most wonderful garden story in the world, because it is set in a desert. Lovely that you know it too."

He emptied his coffee. "My house is in good hands with you. So is the garden. It's got a bit out of shape, but I'm sure you are going to take care of it without chainsaw or landscape gardener."

Eli nodded. Mr. Meyer took a little piece of paper, wrote a number on it and pushed it towards Marcus. "It's yours for this."

"You're not serious!" Marcus passed the note over to Eli. She, too, could not believe what was written on it. For a moment she felt unreserved joy, but then reason prevailed and she handed back the piece of paper.

"We cannot accept this."

Mr. Meyer smiled. "Yes you can."

He stood up and shook his head when Eli wanted to help him clear the table. "I enjoy being still independent."

It sounded sad. Eli pondered whether he possibly wanted to retain the right of residence in the house? With a price like that, there had to be a drawback somewhere!

"I suggest, we make an appointment at the solicitors first thing tomorrow", he said as if reading her mind. "My son would have to travel six hundred kilometres to get here. He's never going to make it." Despite his wrinkles and white hair he suddenly looked like a little rascal.

"May I ask you your first name?" Eli asked.

"Will. Why?"

Eli swallowed; the time machine had catapulted her back to the present without any warning. She suddenly saw an old widower in front of her who was forced to sell his house because he had to move into a home, and who just happened to be called Meyer - to be honest, she did not even know whether old Mrs. Meyer had spelled her name with an e or an a, with an i or a y. Mr. Meyer had been married for a long time and he had loved his garden. It meant a lot to him to give his house to someone who would appreciate it and not level it to the ground. That was really not that extraordinary. His wife had been called Millie. It could be a pet name for Emily, but could stand just as well for Mildred. Mildred Meyer - a name that was probably as common as old cherry trees in suburban gardens. In former times, people used to have their own apples, pears and cherries and quite a few fruit trees had survived the invasion of conifers from modern landscaping. And everyone knew the fairy tale of the little prince. Alright, except Marcus. He preferred balance sheets to popular fiction. That was the reason he got on really well with Emma.

Eli held her right hand out to Mr. Meyer. "I promise to look after your garden for you."

Marcus smiled. "And I will look after the house."

"I know." Will Meyer squeezed Eli's hand. "My Millie always said: we are only visitors and before we go we have to make sure that whatever we love will pass into good hands." His wrinkles started to dance. "If you ever have children, tell them the story of the little prince. And the one about the old garden."

Eli's pocket rang. A text message. *Great you like the garden. Have found mine over here, too: view from the office over Central Park! Regards to M. Emma.* Eli held her mobile out for Marcus to read; he grinned.

"Her tip was great, wasn't it?"

The house sale took a little longer than planned, but finally the son could not fight against his father's will, even the grandchildren tried in vain to stop their grandfather from wasting their inheritance. Mr. Meyer told them all about it a few weeks later whilst they were sitting

in the solicitor's office and then put on his most beautiful rascal-smile.

He moved in to the home, but only for a few days. They said he passed away peacefully; Eli did not go to the funeral. She visited him in the cemetery a little later. The gravestone had not yet been set. A simple wooden cross adorned the grave covered with withered flowers: *William Otto Meyer*.

Eli looked up to the cloudy late autumn sky. She had known all along, and she did not care if it was possible or not. She knelt by the grave and smiled as she dug a hole in the ground. She took the rusty little chimney from the pocket of her coat, put it in and covered it carefully. She thought of the garden. She should put snowdrops in front of the wall, and loads of mint. Later, she was going to look for a gnarly root to put beside her new pond. At some point the frogs' croaks would mix with Luigi's funny tooting and she would find Nick again. Beneath the leaves or in winter with a cap of snow or in the middle of the unfurling ferns in Spring – but at the very latest spitting cherry stones next summer.

To be sure!

Mrs. Meyer's Nettle Soup

(serves four)

Ingredients:

A large bowl of nettle leaves (harvest using gloves); add ground
elder, sorrel, wood sorrel, violet leaves, daisy leaves and/or a
few dandelion leaves for taste.
¾ litre of water
¼ litre of milk
2 tbsp. butter
2 onions (or spring onions accordingly)
1 – 2 cloves of garlic, 1 lovage leaf
Instant vegetable stock. Salt, pepper, nutmeg
½ – 1 cup of whipping cream to taste
1 – 3 tsp cornflower starch if necessary
4 tsp natural yoghurt
A few stalks of parsley or chives

Preparation:

Chop onions and fry in butter; wash nettle leaves and pull off
the coarse stalks (same with all other leaves), add the crushed
garlic and the lovage leaf. As soon as the leaves start softe-
ning, add water and milk, season with salt, pepper and vegetable stock and simmer for about 10 minutes until leaves are
soft. Puree everything. Should the soup not be thick enough,
briefly bring to a boil again, mix the starch with cold water to
a smooth paste and stir in. Mix in lightly whipped cream and
divide into 4 dishes; in the centre of each plate, place one
spoonful of yoghurt, sprinkle with chopped herbs and some
freshly ground nutmeg.

Serve with fresh bread, butter and salt.

Longing is the beginning of all change.

Anselm Grün

Why I had to write this book

Some stories seem to come from nowhere, start nesting in your thoughts without asking; others develop from a vague idea, guarded and incubated just like a raw egg, until a naked chick hatches, looking for warmth in the carefully built nest. *Mrs. Meyer's Magical Garden* has a bit of both: suddenly, the idea was there, buzzing around in my head for more than a year; turned-over and rotated numerous times.

Silly thoughts, the brain criticised. *Write it down,* the stomach recommended. I listened to my stomach and as with all stories you take from privacy to the public, the brain helped to structure it, revise it and tell it for readers and not just for myself.

I grew up in a village and our house had a large garden which was a pleasure garden in the very best sense of the word: we lived from the fruit it produced, carrots, turnips, rhubarb, berries of all kinds and also lettuce and herbs; there was a bed with mint, the leaves of which were dried in the attic in autumn. I remember huge tubs of spinach that would fit in a few freezer bags after cooking and pureeing. And the meticulously covered strawberry field from which we were not allowed to nibble because everything was going to be preserved and made into jam. In my mother's garden there were also flowers, mostly the kind that returned every year or ones you could collect the seeds of; there was no money for expensive arrangements. The marigolds with their bright colours more than made up for it.

There were also trees in my childhood garden, plums, mirabelle, apples – but one thing was missing, which I most longed for: a cherry tree. Although this garden was mostly a kitchen garden, we did not just sow, weed and harvest. With my mother, I walked there daily from bed to bed and every day there was something new to discover. It is this particular memory that I have carried with me and wherever I lived, I always had a little green kingdom for myself, even if it was just one metre of windowsill or four square metres of balcony.

It took many years until I could finally call a real garden my own after buying our house. Measured by the country gardens of my childhood, it is not large, though compared to the bath towel-sized gardens of the common terraced houses, it is. And there is an old cherry tree in the middle of it.

In spring it rains petals, half-ripe cherries in summer, masses of leaves in autumn and the paths and beds underneath it are never clean. Nevertheless, I love this tree and I am happy about every blossom, every leaf and about the sweet fruit it still bears. It is an old tree and is sick. Every year a few branches die, there is fungus all over, nothing can be done, the specialist says. And: *get rid of it!*

I would not dream of getting rid of it and instead I allow ivy to climb up, slowly changing it into a magical tree. One can suspect it: Eli's story has its origin in my own garden experiences.

I particularly like the little things in my green retreat and, like in my mother's garden, there is something new to be seen, smelled, tasted and heard every day: the blackbirds singing from the rooftop, building their nests in every possible and impossible place, bathing in the little stream with the water splashing, unconcerned by human observers. Feathery cotton grass, swaying in the wind, the aroma of herbs and lemons, the taste of sun-ripened tomatoes, the rustling of the hedgehogs announcing the evening, the silent flight of bats around the conservatory at night.

For twelve years I nurtured and maintained my garden until the diggers came – unlike Eli, we had commissioned them ourselves. The restructuring of our house inevitably involved a restructuring of the garden and I used the destruction to fulfil my wish for a pond including a stream, and we built a bench around the old cherry tree.

During restructuring I had already started writing an internet garden diary, not primarily describing the work (which I have, like any other gardener) but the diversity and sensuality that can be created and enjoyed even in a small garden.

My camera is a constant companion during my tours and I am happy that my garden-picture-tours give more than just a visual impression of the trees, leaves and blossoms to the visitors of my blog. The following entry shows that I have toyed with the thought for quite a while, to combine both my passion for gardening and writing.

When „Die Detektivin" was first published, the following Asian proverb was printed on the publisher's brochure: „A book is like a garden you carry in your pocket". This is my motto for reading and I would like it to be my motto for writing, too: a story that will let you, dear readers, feel the wind in the grass or the dry leaves; find words that will conjure-up the scent of an old rose in your nose, that create a world as colourful as a carpet of forget-me-nots and marsh marigolds, weaved near the banks of a pond by the warmth of spring, but not omitting the grey, poured over the land by a November sky. And in the midst of this garden which grows and flowers, wilts, withers and resurrects, my heroes love and suffer, just as in real life: only, they might love and suffer a little more because that is what happens in fictional stories. No publisher in this world – no matter how much he loves the garden motto – would allow me to write a gardening book within a crime story. Well, I would not even allow it myself. But here I can take a chance!

(Blog entry of June 25, 2006, edited excerpt)

Taking that step from net to paper had a most unpleasant background. Five years ago, out of nowhere, I suffered a pulmonary embolism, was thrown from my daily routine, had to stay at home for months and was suddenly able to enjoy things that had become lost within the hectic of a fulfilling everyday working life: I found time in the garden, in the true sense of the word.

At some point during that time, the original version of *Mrs. Meyer's Magical Garden* evolved. Luigi, the funny locomotive, was there from the beginning, although at that point he did not have a name and somehow it also did not fit into a garden story. Lots of other things did not fit either. I was not a little girl anymore and my parents were not divorced but had died a long time ago. Also, the memory of my mother's garden is neither sad nor longing because my own garden has fulfilled all my wishes.

In my day job, I am occupied with people perceiving, handling and eva-luating their surroundings in different ways, the fact is that the truth, so highly valued, ends up being no more than subjectively tinted reality: the causes for errors in testimonies and possible motives for lying are a key issue of interrogation theory. Children love to fantasise, and sometimes it is hard to draw the line. This is unfortunate for the investigating detective; however, for the author it was reason and inspiration for telling the story about *Mrs. Meyer's Magical Garden* from a child's perspective.

We don't see the things the way they are, we see them, the way we are: that is not only the essence of my novel, but also a fitting quote for my interrogation technique seminars.

Originally, the title was supposed to be *Der alte Garten (The old Garden)* but research showed that someone else had the same idea earlier – much earlier! I knew neither text nor author but that changed very quickly. I read with satisfaction that it was a magical story, but it was not mine. And I noticed with surprise that ever returning thoughts and desires will move people to tell a story, even if – as in the case of *Der alte Garten* – they may not be published during the author's lifetime, according to her wish. *Der alte Garten* influenced *Mrs. Meyer's Magical Garden,* just as experiences and adventures do, which not only leave their mark in life, but also in stories. *The little Prince, The secret Garden* and *Momo* are amongst my favourite books, especially *Momo*, this wonderful story about time, and: yes, I love fairy tales! The ones by Hans Christian Andersen, the brothers Grimm and Astrid Lindgren. Why did *Ronia the Robber's Daughter,* of all stories, stumble into Mrs. Meyer's garden? The genie in a bottle that sent me Eli, may know ...

Artists and their gardens have always fascinated me, Claude Monet and his water lily paradise in Giverny, Hannah Höch, the well-known Dadaist, who passionately admitted: *Ich verreise in meinen Garten (I travel to my Garden),* the summer residence of the painter Max Liebermann, at home in Berlin like Hannah Höch, or the magical Garden Rooms, which the author Vita Sackville-West and her husband Harold Nicolson created at Sissinghurst Castle in Kent. Until this day, these gardens attract numerous visitors from around the world, but even just knowing them from books and pictures, it is not difficult to imagine that their magic is mainly created by the personalities of those who conceived and created them. People who start gardening often never get away from it, and the fact that there are a lot of artists among them reveals that gardeners and artists are very much alike. The one, as well as the other, needs to be an expert of his trade, has to have knowledge of the correct techniques and the ability to plan things. At the same time, they have to be able to forget their knowledge and plans and be open for the new and unexpected, leave room for intuition, fantasy and creativity.

One can have splendid disputes, not only about the beauty of art but also about beautiful gardens: some like accurate beds, minimalism and the geometry of flowers, others enthuse about abundant originality, and so a garden always reflects the thoughts and feelings of the people living in and with it.

Others may like my garden, but they would also do things a little or some-times even a lot different. Like every piece of art, it is more than colour and material, gardens are more than just green. And that is why I have written this book: to tell about the colours of fantasy, about the magic of fairy tales and about the child inside us all that wakes up and dreams and longs as soon as we enter an old garden.

Winter 2015

PS: There really are five-leaved clovers, and every year I harvest those co-lourful tomatoes from Eli's rainbow bed, and Nick does not lounge by the cherry tree (because from our bench he would not be able to see much) but near an old lilac bush. And his name is spelled with c only.

Remarks about the Aphorisms

Page 7 *(Someone who hears butterflies laugh ...)*
Quote from the song of the same name (lyrics: Carlo Karges, music: Lutz Rahn) by the rock group Novalis. *Wer Schmetterlinge lachen hört* was a reminiscence to the poet Friedrich Freiherr von Hardenberg aka Novalis (1772 – 1801) and a free interpretation of his poem *Es färbte sich die Wiese grün (With Colour Blooms the Meadow Green)*. Use of this quote by the kind permission of Gary Karges and SMV Schacht Musikverlage GmbH & Co.KG.

Page 9 *(Omnium rerum principia parva sunt.)*
Marcus Tullius Cicero (106 v. Chr. – 43 v. Chr.), Roman politician, lawyer, poet, philosopher – and Rome's most famous speaker. Source: *De finibus* (5,58); translated literally: „The beginnings of all things are small."

Page 43 *(A man who does not think by himself ...)*
Oscar Fingal O'Flahertie Wills Wilde (1854 – 1900), Irish poet. Nick would have loved Oscar Wilde's sentence: „To do nothing at all is the most difficult thing in the world, the most difficult and the most intellectual." *(The Critic as Artist; scene 2/Gilbert)*

Page 73 *(The highest goal that man can achieve ...)*
Johann Wolfgang von Goethe (1749 – 1832) was not only a writer; from about 1780 he systematically dealt with scientific problems. Among other things, he wanted to deliver *A History of the Human Spirit in a Nutshell,* as mentioned in a letter to Wilhelm von Humboldt in 1798. He was particularly interested in the sensual-moral effect of colours and he increasingly shifted his analyses to the field of psychology.

Page 107 *(If you think of angels ...)*
Unfortunately, I do not know the exact source.

Page 143 *(We don't see the things the way they are ...)*
This quote also circulates in a slightly modified version; mainly the Talmud is stated as the source, unfortunately always without exact reference. Additionally, French poet Anaïs Nin (1903 – 1977) is mentioned as the author, again without

any evidence. Some authors mention the source as unknown. According to my research, the Talmud seems to be the most likely source.

Page 144 *(Se non è vero ...)*

Giordano Bruno (1548 – 1600), Italian philosopher and poet; reference: *Über die heroischen Leidenschaften II, 3 (About heroic passion)*; G. Bruno was sentenced to be burnt at the stake and executed in 1600 after eight years of imprisonment for heresy and practising magic. His books were on the index of forbidden books until 1966; only in 2000 did the Catholic Church declared the execution to have been unjust, however, without fully rehabilitating him.

Page 138 *(Longing is the beginning ...)*

Father Dr. Anselm Grün, born 1945, cellarar of the Münster-Schwarzach monastery since 1977 and author of several spiritual books. The quote is from: *Anselm Grün, Einfach nur leben! (Just live!), Verlagsgruppe Weltbild, Augsburg, 2010, p. 10 (Lebenskraft Sehnsucht. Wandlung)*. In the same text later on: „Change (...) does not work with noise (...) Because whatever grows, does not make a noise. If we calmly accept the things the way they really are (...) then the miracles, described in many fairytales, may happen." I think this is a closing remark, both beautiful and fitting for the story of Eli and Mrs. Meyer's magical garden. Reprinted by kind permission of Father Anselm Grün.

Reference

With the exception of the ones below, all photographs used in this book show motives from my garden, taken in the years 1992 – 2012, some of them artistically arranged. The window frame on the front and back covers I photographed in 2011 in the Spandau citadel and then edited it. The pictures in the background were taken in my own garden. The clover leaf (p. 143) is a discovery from my diary. © Nikola Hahn.

Nicodemus has been looking after my garden for many years. I bought him at "Gärtner Pötschke" in 41561 Kaarst; www.poetschke.de („Nicodemus"). Photo reprinted courtesy of Gärtner Pötschke.

The photo on p. 162 I took in Max Liebermann's garden at Wannsee in Berlin upon my visit on May 14, 2011. It shows the famous „Birkenweg" (path between birch trees) which served as the painter's motive on numerous occasions. Reprint courtesy of Max-Liebermann-Gesellschaft Berlin e.V., www.liebermann-villa.de; for the photo: © N. Hahn.

Matt's Forest, the rumphobs, dark trolls, grey gnomes and the unique idea to practise not being afraid, Eli aka Ronia the Robber's Daughter has taken from Astrid Lindgren's fairy tale of the same name, which Pa not only told her but he also lived: Astrid Lindgren, *Ronia Räubertochter (Ronia the Robber's Daughter)*, © Verlag Friedrich Oetinger, Hamburg, 1982/2000; Use of names/terms by kind permission of the copyright holder.

One of Eli's favourite stories is the fairy tale *Der alte Garten (The old Garden)*, which Pa had to read to her three times in succession. So it is no surprise she literally remembers a passage from the story when she visits Mrs. Meyer's garden for the last time to say farewell. The quotes (p. 139/140) are taken from: Marie Luise Kaschnitz, *Der alte Garten. Ein Märchen*, 1990, S. 155, 158; reprinted by kind permission of the copyright holder.

Mrs. Meyer recounts the story of the little prince freely based on Antoine de Saint Exupéry's book, while Eli and Mr. Meyer (p. 151) quote literally from the following edition: Antoine de Saint-Exupéry, *Der kleine Prinz*, Lizenzausgabe C. Bertelsmann,

Gütersloh, o. J., p. 107. Reprint of the quotes by kind permission of the copyright holder, © 1950 and 2008, Karl Rauch Verlag, Düsseldorf.

Of course snowdrops also grow in my garden, and every year I am happy to see those cheeky bunches of little bells appear in impossible places and start ringing in spring, unperturbed by the cold and the snow. However, I was unaware of the fact that there are about five hundred different kinds of snowdrops setting collector's hearts racing. Mrs. Meyer could explain the different crown markings to Eli because Marion Lagoda wrote an article about them. *Das Fest der Schneeglöckchen (The Snowdrops' Feast)*, in: kraut&rüben, magazine 2/2008, S. 4 – 9.

The story about the snowdrops' colour was not told to Eli by Grandma Mary, but was told to me by my mother when I was a child. The complete story (plus two more) can be found in: Nikola Hahn (2009, 2013), *Wie das Schneeglöckchen zu seiner Farbe kam. Märchen – Bilder (How the Snowdrop got its colour. Fairytales – Pictures)*, Thoni Verlag, Rödermark.

For the Book butterfly in all variations © Sandra Nabbefeld; details: www.thoni-verlag.eu/impressum-kontakt-quellen/bildnachweis/

Bibliographic information about the books described on pages 159/160 in the order in which they are mentioned:

Nikola Hahn, *Die Detektivin (The Detective;* Nikola Hahns crime novel about the history of criminology) published 1998 by Marion von Schröder-Verlag, Munich; new edition: Berlin 2011 (Ullstein)

Marie Luise Kaschnitz, *Der alte Garten. Ein Märchen (The old Garden. A Fairytale),* Munich 1990 (dtv)

Antoine de Saint-Exupéry, *Der kleine Prinz (The little Prince),* Düsseldorf 1956 (Karl Rauch)

Frances Hodgson Burnett, *Der geheime Garten (The secret Garden),* illustrated by Inga Moore, 3rd edition, Stuttgart 2009 (Urachhaus)

Michael Ende, *Momo. Ein Märchen-Roman (Momo),* Stuttgart, o. O. (K. Thienemanns)

Astrid Lindgren, *Ronja Räubertochter (Ronia the Robber's Daughter),* Hamburg 1982/2000 (Friedrich Oetinger)

Horst Keller, *Monets Jahre in Giverny: Ein Garten wird Malerei (Monet's years living in Giverny: A Garden becomes a Painting),* Köln 2001 (DuMont)

Gesine Sturm, Johannes Bauersachs, *Ich verreise in meinen Garten. Der Garten der Hannah Höch (I travel to my Garden. Hanna Höch's Garden),* Berlin 2007 (Stapp)

Jenns Eric Howoldt, Uwe M. Schneede (Hg.), *Im Garten von Max Liebermann, (In the Garden of Max Liebermann),* Hamburger Kunsthalle, Staatliche Museen zu Berlin, 2nd edition 2004 (book on the exhibition „Im Garten von Max Liebermann", Hamburger Kunsthalle/Alte Nationalgalerie Berlin 2004/2005)

Julia Bachstein (Hg.), Vita Sackville-West und Harold Nicolson and others, *Sissinghurst. Portrait eines Gartens (Sissinghurst. A Portrait),* Frankfurt 2006 (Insel)

„Gärten sind mehr als grün" (Gardens are more than just green), Dr. Andrea Friedrich, Milton Keynes, England, in: Der Spiegel 30/2009 (Briefe; Letters)

A heartfelt Thankyou ...

... to Christine in Central Hesse: for your lovely mail with lots of exclamation marks; to Switzerland to Fabienne for your wonderful reader's comments, to Dieter from the Taunus for his structural assistance, to Mrs. Bünger and Mrs. Seeßle, in Frankfurt and Offenbach in representation of everyone who test read Mrs. Meyer's Magical Garden and encouraged me to go ahead with the project, even though that meant that they had to wait even longer for a new crime story from Old Frankfurt.

As always, an especially big thankyou goes to Thomas – my first and toughest critic for the last twenty-five years.

Also, I was very pleased with Wolfram Franke's praise, author and publisher of the gardening magazine „kraut & rüben"– and, last but not least: thanks to Birger in Lund/Sweden for your critique and the funny story about Astrid Lindgren.

www.ingramcontent.com/pod-product-compliance
Lightning Source LLC
Chambersburg PA
CBHW020654260626
47157CB00008B/3029